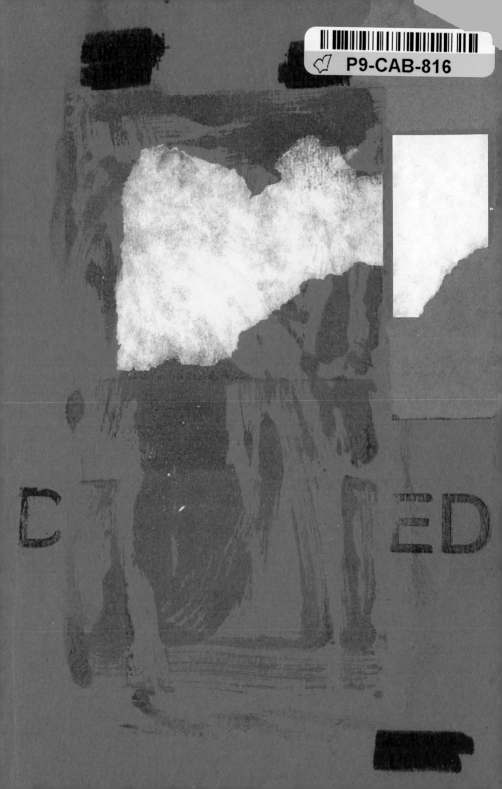

a wonderful,
terrible time

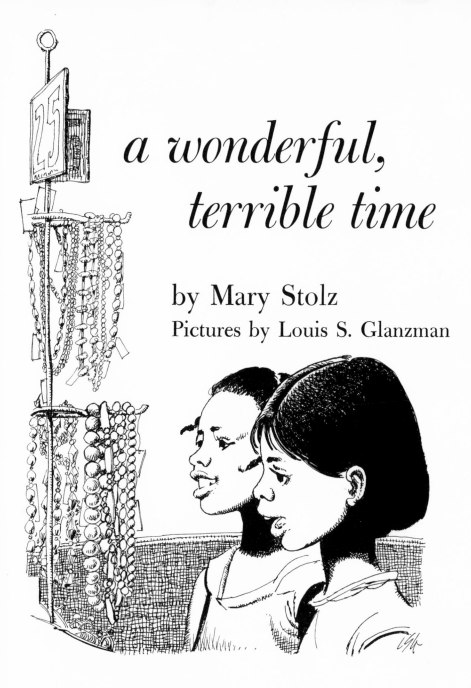

a wonderful, terrible time

by Mary Stolz
Pictures by Louis S. Glanzman

HARPER & ROW, PUBLISHERS · New York, Evanston, and London

A WONDERFUL, TERRIBLE TIME
Text copyright © 1967 by Mary Stolz
Pictures copyright © 1967 by Louis S. Glanzman

For B. A. D.

Some Other Books by Mary Stolz

AND LOVE REPLIED

THE BEAUTIFUL FRIEND AND OTHER STORIES

BECAUSE OF MADELINE

THE BULLY OF BARKHAM STREET

THE DAY AND THE WAY WE MET

A DOG ON BARKHAM STREET

FRÉDOU

GOOD-BY MY SHADOW

HOSPITAL ZONE

IN A MIRROR

THE NOONDAY FRIENDS

THE ORGANDY CUPCAKES

PIGEON FLIGHT

PRAY LOVE, REMEMBER

READY OR NOT

ROSEMARY

THE SEAGULLS WOKE ME

SECOND NATURE

SOME MERRY-GO-ROUND MUSIC

TO TELL YOUR LOVE

WAIT FOR ME, MICHAEL

Chapter One

Summer.

The sun was so hot, so bright, that shade had nowhere to go except in the alleys with the trash cans and the cats and the clothes hanging slack on the lines.

Mady Guthrie and Sue Ellen Forrest sat on the stoop in front of their apartment building and watched boys kill one another in the street.

"Bang, bang, bang!"

A boy screamed, staggered, fell to the ground. Then he jumped to his feet, aimed a finger at his assassin.

1

"Bang, bang! Bang, bang, bang!"

"You're dead."

"Now you're dead!"

They killed up and down the street, on the sidewalks, on the steps of buildings, in and out of the alleys.

Bang, bang, bang, bang! They filled the summer air with invisible bullets that never missed their mark.

Sue Ellen and Mady watched, yawning.

A cat walked by, sat down, and watched them. Then it too yawned and walked into the alley to be cool where the shade was.

Their last year's teacher, Miss Rice, came down the street. She carried a rose-colored umbrella against the sun and looked different from her classroom self.

"Hi, teach," said Mady and Sue Ellen together.

Miss Rice looked at them and took a second to remember who they were. Then she said, "Sue Ellen. Mady. How are you? What are you doing?"

"Nothing."

"Can't you think of something to do?"

"We will," said Sue Ellen.

"Later," said Mady.

Miss Rice walked on. She had been a pretty good teacher, the kind who could keep a whole class in its seat when the lesson was going on. She did it just

2

with a look. In some classes the kids wandered all around and the teacher didn't know what to do about it. But Miss Rice just looked, and all the children stayed where they belonged and learned something.

Just the same, a new teacher lay ahead now, and Miss Rice was out of their lives. Sue Ellen and Mady forgot her as she rounded the corner.

"Let's play hopscotch," said Sue Ellen.

There was an old blue hopscotch game, almost wiped out, on the sidewalk in front of them. They had drawn it themselves, in blue chalk, days ago. It was almost gone from feet walking on it but was still clear enough to see.

They played, hopping from box to box, using a bunch of safety pins for throwing.

"It's too hot," Sue Ellen decided after a while.

"Okay," said Mady.

They sat on the stoop again, watching the boys, who never seemed to get too hot to kill one another.

Down at the end of the block a fireman appeared. As soon as he came, children gathered like flies around a melon. Some of them already had bathing suits on, as if they'd known he was going to come and put the sprinkler on the hydrant for children to splash.

"Oh, boy," said Sue Ellen. "Let's play in the water."

"We don't have any bathing suits."

"We'll wear old shorts and shirts. We'll ask my momma."

Mady's mother worked. She was a nurse at a nearby hospital. But Sue Ellen's mother stayed home and kept house. Sue Ellen's father was a taxi driver. Mady's father was dead.

They ran upstairs into Sue Ellen's apartment, where Mrs. Forrest was ironing clothes, wiping the sweat off her forehead.

"Whew," she said cheerfully, as the girls burst through the door. "What a job. You know, one day you'll go through that door without opening it. Then we'll have to pay to get a new one."

"Can we put on old shorts and shirts and play in the fire hydrant?" Sue Ellen shouted. "The fireman just opened it. It's only half an hour, Momma. They only leave it open half an hour."

"Has he got the sprinkler on it?"

"Oh, yes. Can we?"

"Well, I don't know."

"Oh, boy, thanks," said Sue Ellen and tore into the bedroom. Mady followed.

"She didn't say Yes."

"She said 'I don't know.' You know that means Yes. If she means No she says 'No,' or 'Ask your father.' You go get your things on too."

Mady had two keys to her apartment, which was

4

just across the hall. You had to open the door twice. Once with the key to the old lock, and once with the key to the bolt her mother had had put on. Mrs. Guthrie said roughneck elements ruled the neighborhood. She said that Mrs. Forrest, who sometimes forgot to lock her door at all, was foolhardy.

Mady used her two keys and went in. The apartment, in the middle of the day, was tidy and silent and strange. The blinds were drawn, and the clock on the kitchen cabinet ticked rapidly to itself. Mady always had the feeling that it sounded cross, as if it were going *tut-tut-tut-tut-tut,* and would have shaken its head if it could.

The apartment was nice and cool.

Mady hurried, getting into her oldest shorts and shirt. Sue Ellen was waiting in the hall outside. Together they ran down to the street. They leaped shouting and laughing into the clear, sparkling, bubbling spray from the hydrant. Eyes closed, they shoved their faces into the fizz and froth of the water, getting their hair drenched, and their clothes.

It was marvelous. Mady stamped with pleasure. She decided it was like being in Niagara Falls.

"Niagara Falls! Niagara Falls!" she shouted above the din. "We're all in Niagara Falls!"

A boy doubled up, holding his knees to his chest, and rolled about. "I'm going over Niagara Falls in a barrel!" he yelled.

"Niagara Falls! Niagara Falls! Niagara, Niagara, Ni—Ni—agara—agara!" The children sang and shouted.

After a while the fireman came to turn the hydrant off. He stood with the wrench in his hand, watching the children and smiling. He looked as if he wanted to get into the rushing water with them.

But in a few minutes he said, "Sorry, kids, that's all for today," and turned off Niagara Falls with his wrench.

Sopping, soaking, dripping, Mady and Sue Ellen sloshed down the street back to their apartment building.

"For goodness' sake, go into the bathroom and change," said Mrs. Forrest. "You'll flood us out." But she sounded lively, as if the sight of them, smiling and dripping, made her happy.

Mady went across the hall, used her two keys again, and after she'd dried herself in the bathroom and got into her dress, took the towel and wiped up the floor. Her mother tried to keep things nice and was not as cheery and chirpy as Mrs. Forrest. Which was why Mady usually played in Sue Ellen's apartment and not the other way around.

Mrs. Forrest had finished the ironing. She said that now she had to go marketing and do some other things and did the girls want to go with her.

"What are the other things?" asked Sue Ellen.

"Oh, you know. I'll visit a few people. It's summer. No need to hurry. I'll have some lemonade with Mrs. Gerez, most likely."

Sue Ellen and Mady decided they'd stay home.

"We'll have a lemonade party for our dolls," said Sue Ellen.

"That's a good idea," said her mother. "You'll find cookies in the cupboard, in case the dolls are hungry." She blew them a kiss.

"Bye, Momma."

"Bye, Aunt Lillian."

Mady had to go back across the hall and use her two keys all over again. She got her Chinese doll, Kim, her dancing doll, Vera, and her just doll doll, whose name was Sally. Sue Ellen had said she could only invite three, as that was all the room there was. She had only three dolls anyway, and that was all Sue Ellen had. Mrs. Guthrie said that was a lot, and that some little girls didn't have any. But Mady didn't know any girls without a doll.

Sue Ellen had a little round table and six little chairs and a plastic tea set for six. Her father had given them to her for Christmas, and here it was the beginning of July and nothing was broken.

Sue Ellen took better care of her things than Mady did, although Mrs. Forrest never said, "Be careful," and Mady's mother said it all the time.

Well, it was funny, thought Mady, looking at her dancing doll who had lost one leg, and at Sally who looked a sight but was her love. Her Chinese doll

7

was practically perfect but also practically new, since Mady's birthday came at the end of June.

Well, there it was. Some people took better care than other people did. But it was summer, and no time to worry.

Sue Ellen had a baby doll, a boy doll, and a rag doll. The boy doll, Daniel, and the baby doll, who was just called Baby, were as good as new, but the rag doll had burst a seam. Sue Ellen sewed her up carefully, taking a long time, and the party couldn't begin until she was finished.

"I'm going to be a doctor when I grow up," said Sue Ellen, taking tiny stitches. "The kind that sews on people."

"You can't be a doctor," said Mady. "Doctors are men." She stood at the window, looking down at the boys who'd returned to their shooting, except for some who were playing stickball.

"Don't be silly," said Sue Ellen, biting off the thread. "There are lots of lady doctors and lady lawyers and lady policemen and lady taxi drivers and—"

"Lady astronauts," said Mady.

"Only they're Russian. We don't have one. Yet."

"And lady presidents."

"Well, I guess not yet, either," said Sue Ellen. She patted her rag doll. "There you are, Geneva. You're well enough to go to the party. Just don't overdo."

When all the dolls were seated, waiting, Mady and

8

Sue Ellen went to the kitchen. They made a pitcher of pink lemonade, a big one, and then poured some of it into the tiny teapot that went with the plastic tea set. They put some cookies on a plate and broke up some very small pieces to put in front of each doll on a tiny plastic plate.

"Now," said Mady and Sue Ellen together, sitting on the floor. "Now, let's have the party."

Sue Ellen poured lemonade from the little teapot into the tiny teacups. She gave each doll a bit of cookie.

They had to talk for their dolls, and the Chinese doll, being the newest, got to speak first.

"Ting, ling, kow foo chop suey," said Kim, the Chinese doll, in Mady's voice but high and singing. "Kow ling chow mein foo!"

"What language you using, man?" said the rag doll in Sue Ellen's voice. "I come from Brooklyn and don't dig you a bit."

"Don't be silly," said Sally, the doll doll, in Mady's voice but deeper now. "He's speaking Chinese."

"Why?" asked Geneva.

"Oh, you are silly. Because he's Chinese, that's why. He comes from Hong Kong. It says so on his shoes," said Mady.

"Well, he isn't in Hong Kong now," said Sue Ellen. "So why doesn't he talk American?"

They had forgotten to use their doll voices, and

9

for a moment they glared at each other, and the tea party was threatened.

Then Sue Ellen shrugged, moved Daniel slightly, and said in her boy-doll voice, "Man, that's the most. A visitor from Hong Kong." When neither Mady nor any of her dolls responded, Sue Ellen had Geneva stand up. "Let's have some of that lemonade," said Geneva. "And these dear little pieces of cookie. I'm hungry."

Mady and Sue Ellen poured their own lemonade and ate their own cookies, and then helped the dolls with theirs. The tea party was saved.

When they'd finished eating, Vera, the dancing doll, said, "I believe now I'll dance." Mady helped her up from the chair. "I will spin on my one leg like a ballerina," said Vera. Mady helped her to spin around the room, while Sue Ellen sang a song her father taught her.

> *Frère Jacques, Frère Jacques,*
> *Dormez-vous? Dormez-vous?*
> *Sonnez les matines, sonnez les matines,*
> *Ding dang dong. Ding dang dong.*

Vera danced for quite a while until Sue Ellen stopped singing and Geneva said, "Can't anybody else do anything?"

"What can you do?" asked Sally, the doll doll.

"I can sing," said Geneva, and sang just the way Sue Ellen had been singing. In fact, she sang the same song.

10

"Well, I've had enough of this," said Sally. "I want to do something too."

"Dada dada dada," said the baby doll.

"Let's go on a freedom march," said Daniel.

All the dolls got up, gathered into their owners' arms, and they stamped around the living room on their owners' feet, singing.

We shall overcome, we shall overcome,
We shall overcome some day!

"Martin Luther King is up there," said Daniel.

"Where? Where?" asked Vera, leaping high in the air.

"He's out of sight at the head of the parade. We're following him," said Daniel.

"Freedom now! Freedom now!" shouted all the dolls, even the Chinese doll and the baby doll.

They used Mady's and Sue Ellen's voices and Mady's and Sue Ellen's legs, and they stamped and shouted all around the room.

Suddenly, from underneath, there was a banging noise.

The dolls stopped marching. So did Sue Ellen and Mady. The banging noise came from the woman who lived downstairs. She was poking the ceiling with her broom, telling them to keep quiet and if they didn't they'd be sorry.

Sue Ellen and Mady knew the whole message, just

11

from how the broom banged. They decided to keep quiet.

The dolls went back to the table, and their hostesses sat on the floor beside them. They finished up the lemonade and the last cookie.

"Would you go on a freedom march?" Mady asked Sue Ellen. "A real one?"

"How could I go on a freedom march? I'm too young."

"There are some kids go. Or they sit-in or pray-in. You know. Some of them even get in jail."

Mady's own father had been in jail in Mississippi. He had gone down to that state to get Negroes to register for voting and he hadn't ever come back, because one night he'd been shot, and he died. Mady didn't say anything about this now to Sue Ellen, but she thought that Sue Ellen could have mentioned something about it, just to show that she remembered Mady had had a father too, once upon a time.

But all Sue Ellen said was, "Well, I'm too young," in a stubborn voice.

"Well, but if you *weren't*, would you?" Mady persisted.

Sue Ellen narrowed her eyes, thinking. She'd seen on television what the freedom marches and the protests and the boycotts and the voter registration drives were like. Colored people being beat up and yelled at. Dogs biting them. Policemen hitting them on the head with clubs. She'd seen little kids with whole bunches of white grown-ups screaming at them because they wanted to go to school someplace. Or their parents wanted them to. Or the government did. It was awful, all those grown-up people hollering at those little kids.

Momma, when she saw it, said it was awful too. "But terrible things do happen in life, Sue Ellen," she'd said. "And they don't always happen to other people. And they don't always happen down South, either."

But Sue Ellen didn't want to think about it. She wanted to be safe and warm with Pop and Momma, with Mady and Mrs. Guthrie, with her friends from school and the teachers she had there that were nice, which all of them weren't, but some were.

Poor Mady's own father had got himself killed in a voter registration drive, but Sue Ellen didn't ever mention that to her because it might make her sad. Sue Ellen did not like people to be sad.

"I don't want to think about it," she said now to Mady. "Anyway, when we grow up," she added confidently, "it will all be over. There won't be any freedom marches or sit-ins or like that. Martin Luther King will fix it."

Mady sighed. Sue Ellen was her very best friend, but there was one thing you couldn't ever do with her and that was talk about anything serious. Especially not anything serious and sad too. Mady thought that being a Negro was both sad and serious lots of the time, but Sue Ellen just wouldn't talk about it.

"Well, it was a nice tea party," said Mady, "but I think the dolls are tired out now. They ought to go to bed."

"Yes, especially the baby doll," said Sue Ellen. "She's got that grouchy look she gets when she's overtired."

So Mady went back across the hall, using her keys for the fourth time, and gently put her dolls to bed on the windowsill all in a row on a blanket. Usually she just tossed them into a chair or even on the floor, until her mother told her to pick them up. But she had decided to be a better mother to her dolls from now on.

She felt sorry about Vera's lost leg and about Sally's battered appearance. The doll doll looked as if she had a permanent case of chicken pox, or had been left out on the fire escape in the rain, which, as it happened, was what *had* happened.

But what was past was past, as her mother often said. The thing was to do better from now on. Having decided this, she immediately felt better. Mady always felt better when she'd decided something, even if she hardly ever did what she'd decided.

Mostly, she realized, she did what Sue Ellen decided.

Chapter Two

Summers were best of all. In any case Sue Ellen and Mady thought they were. It wasn't being out of school that pleased them best. For two years now they'd been going to school in a brand new building. The principal, Mr. Carmondy, was a man everybody liked, and so far Sue Ellen and Mady had been in the same class together and had had teachers they liked.

Lots of the kids around here absolutely hated school and were just waiting to get old enough to be dropouts. But Sue Ellen and Mady liked school and didn't intend to be dropouts ever.

Still, being free—the way you were in summertime, just completely free to do anything you wanted, or not do it—was marvelous. And Mady, who hated the cold, loved the way she could dash in and out of the apartment in the summertime. No jackets or boots or ice-crusted mittens. No freezing fingers when the mittens got lost.

In July, when people went around complaining about the heat and humidity, Mady just smiled and wished it would go on forever.

Sue Ellen's father, Mr. Forrest, who had gone to college for a couple of years and knew, Mady figured, just about more than anyone else did, even people who'd *finished* college, had said that Mady was a salamander.

"What's that?" Sue Ellen had asked jealously.

"Sort of a lizard. The Greeks believed it could live in the heart of the fire and not burn up."

Mady had wondered if she really liked being compared to a lizard, but Mr. Forrest, seeing her expression, had laughed. "It's a beautiful little slender creature, silky and swift," he'd told her.

Winters around here sometimes the furnaces went off and the apartments got cold, icy cold as the out-of-doors. That, to Mady, was horrible. The hottest of sultry days and nights were better. Oh, she loved the summertime, and Sue Ellen did too.

The trouble was that being free to do anything you wanted, or not do it, left you after a few weeks

16

not sure sometimes what it was you wanted to do, or not do.

"What'll we do now?" Mady asked Sue Ellen when she'd put her dolls away on the windowsill and had returned to Sue Ellen's apartment.

Sue Ellen looked at the clock. Still pretty early. Her mother wouldn't be home probably for ages yet. Her father was due back at four o'clock, but that was a couple of hours off.

"Let's go walk around the ten-cent store."

"Did your momma say it's all right to?" Mady asked.

"She says if we stay together, like always. Did your momma?"

"She says do what Aunt Lillian says, as long as I'm with you, only be careful."

"Well, we're careful," Sue Ellen said impatiently. "I mean, my gosh, do you want a policeman to go with us?"

"I wouldn't mind," said Mady, and Sue Ellen laughed. "We don't have any money," Mady added.

"We never have any money. Hardly ever. They don't charge for walking around."

The ten-cent store was seven blocks away, and by the end of their walk they were glad to get inside. It was air-conditioned. Mady liked air-conditioning because like the spray from the hydrant it was a sign of summer. Besides, you knew that when you went back on the street it would be hot again.

The two girls thought that a ten-cent store was about the best place in the world. Except maybe that outdoor swimming pool where the whole class had been taken just before school let out. They had gone on a subway and neither of them had any idea now of where it was.

But it had been neat, all right. They'd worn rented gray bathing suits, had hot dogs and Coke, and splashed around in this huge pool practically the whole day. Sue Ellen and Mady had to stay in the shallow part because neither of them could swim. But they'd pretended to, going along in the low water, heads up, hands on the bottom, kicking their legs. It had almost felt like swimming, but Mady had had to admit, looking at Sue Ellen humping along, that it didn't really look like swimming.

There had been a slide at the deep end, steep and shining, with water rushing down it. They'd looked at that longingly. Kids were absolutely flying from the top into the pool. Kids that knew how to swim.

Well, they didn't know where that swimming pool was and expected they wouldn't get to go again until next year.

"Can you think as far ahead as next year?" Mady asked now.

Sue Ellen considered. "I guess not. But I can think farther. I can think about being grown up."

"Anybody can do that. It's next year that's hard."

18

They often talked about what they were going to do when they grew up. Mady was going to be like people on television who worked at the zoo and took care of baby animals. Sue Ellen changed her mind all the time. Today she was going to be a doctor. Last week it had been an actress. Sometimes she said she was going to be a teacher and other times an airline hostess. You couldn't tell with Sue Ellen.

They were looking at beautiful colored glass beads and earrings, keeping their hands behind their backs so no one would think they were going to touch.

Ten-cent stores, Mrs. Forrest had told them one day, had spies and cameras all over the place, watching dishonest people.

"We aren't dishonest," Sue Ellen had said. "So they won't be watching us."

"They watch everybody, just in case," Mrs. Forrest had said.

It had made Sue Ellen so angry that for a week she would not go to the ten-cent store at all. But now here she was, looking at the glass beads and earrings, keeping her hands behind her back.

"Where do you suppose the spies and cameras are?" she asked Mady.

They looked around. Nobody looked the least bit spyish, and of course they knew that these days cameras came so small that no one could ever spot them or guess the strange ways they were disguised. They could be in nailheads in the wall, or on the edges of somebody's spectacles. Anywhere.

"Well, I don't like it," Sue Ellen insisted. *"Watching* people. It's awful."

"So do I think so," said Mady. She meant it. Many times when she agreed with Sue Ellen it was because she wanted to be friendly, or didn't disagree, or didn't know whether she did or did not.

"It would be nice to buy something," she said, moving along the counter.

"What would you buy?"

"A goldfish," Mady said promptly. "And a bowl and some colored pebbles and a little castle with a door in it for my fish to swim in and out of."

They went and looked at the goldfish. They were in a great tank of clear water with a column of bubbles rising at one side and a lovely underwater forest arranged for the fish's pleasure. China mermaids and bridges were dotted here and there in the sandy bottom, and a skin diver floated among the fish who wandered through wands of water plants, opening and closing their mouths as if they were saying *ooh, ooh, oooh.*

Some were orange-gold, some yellow-gold, some gold spotted with freckles, and some weren't gold at all. There were a few beautiful black ones with tails like chiffon fans. That's the sort I'd have, thought Mady. A black goldfish.

There were also little green turtles, pushing the water away with tiny clawed feet. They skimmed along the bottom of the tank, then shot almost straight upward to poke their noses—like pencil dots—out of the water for a moment, and then down they went again.

There were snails, moving ever so slowly up the glass sides. They had shining spiral shells and little heads with horns. As the two girls watched, a snail who'd been clinging to a branch of the water plant suddenly let go and drifted down to land in a flurry in the sand.

"I just do love them," said Mady.

"Snails?" asked Sue Ellen, wrinkling her nose.

"Well, I don't exactly love *them*. Except they're all right. No, but the goldfish are gorgeous, aren't they? Especially those black ones with the fan tails."

"Oh, you like all animals," said Sue Ellen.

"So do you," Mady retorted.

"Not the way you do. I mean, I'm not just nuts and crazy over them."

But Mady loved all animals. Cats, dogs, the little gray city sparrows that ate crumbs from her window-sill. What she wanted to see on television was any-thing that had animals in it. The people programs didn't interest her. Sue Ellen, on the other hand, liked Westerns and those terrible ones where you tried to answer questions and win things for answering. Often Sue Ellen could answer the questions better than some of those grown-ups on the program, and she said that one day she was going to go on a program herself. Mady would've died first.

They wandered on.

"What would you buy?" Mady said.

"Huh? Oh, you mean if I could. Well, I guess I'd get my mother one of these aprons, with roses printed on it. Or maybe a dish towel with a map of London, like that one."

Mady wished that she'd said she'd buy her mother something. But she knew that if the time ever came, she'd still get the goldfish and the bowl and the colored pebbles and the little castle.

"Momma would probably like to have a goldfish to look at," she said defensively.

"Sure she would," said Sue Ellen. "Anybody would like a goldfish."

Mady felt somewhat better.

They inspected the pots and pans, passed up tools and nails, stopped in front of the toy counter. They looked for a long time at the different things.

Model cars, and tops, and bags of balloons, and dolls and jeeps and tractors and holsters with guns in them, and marbles and jacks, and painting sets and clay sets, and airplane and warship models, and rockets, and cutout dolls with wardrobes, and—it was almost confusing to look.

23

"What would you buy if you could buy anything here?" said Sue Ellen.

"I'd still buy the goldfish."

"I *said* something *here*."

"I wouldn't buy anything here. I'd buy the goldfish."

"Oh, for goodness' sakes," said Sue Ellen, sounding annoyed.

"What would you?"

Sue Ellen sighed, surveying the entire toy counter. "I guess I'd still buy the apron for my mother."

They laughed at that and went on to inspect the cosmetics, the paper supplies, the ribbon department, the glassware, the candy counter.

Some of the candy looked meltingly good.

"Oh, boy," said Sue Ellen. "Look at the nut rolls."

Mady said, "You know, it's funny, but your mouth really does water when you see something good to eat, doesn't it? I mean, it's not just something people say in books."

Suddenly, in spite of the tea party, they were too hungry to remain looking at candy and cookies, smelling the spicy aroma of hot dogs cooking on a grill, hearing the swish from spigots as ice cream sodas were created.

They left.

Outside, after the coldness of the store, the heat

seemed to swarm at them. Sidewalks glittered with bits of mica, and they could smell hot tar where men had been repairing the street. Several blocks away the elevated train rumbled by, and that sounded hot too, and heavy.

"My goodness," said Sue Ellen. "We'll be cooked before we get home."

Even Mady found it pretty hot, but wouldn't give in and say so.

"Hey girls! Going my way?"

A taxi pulled up to the curb, and there was Sue Ellen's father.

"Hop in," he invited. "I'm on my way to the garage and can just fit in one more fare on my way."

"We can't pay you, driver," said Sue Ellen, climbing into the back seat of the cab. Mady scrambled in after her, feeling pretty sure that everyone was watching them, thinking how lucky they were.

"I'll settle for two smiles and a report on the day's activities," said Mr. Forrest. "What have you two done with yourselves today?"

"Nothing," they said together. And then, "Lots of things."

"We went to Niagara Falls," said Mady.

"And gave a tea party. Elegant, of course," said Sue Ellen.

"Six guests. And dancing."

"We went on a freedom march."

"With Martin Luther King."

"We went shopping for goldfish and aprons and a few other things."

"I don't see any packages," said Mr. Forrest, turning around for a second.

"Practice shopping," Mady explained.

"I see. Pretty good kind at that, I guess," said their chauffeur.

"Not all the time," Sue Ellen said darkly, but then she and her father laughed.

Mady leaned back, blinking. She loved Mr. Forrest. She wished—and when she'd been small, she'd even prayed—that he could be her own father. Now that she was older, she knew what a bad prayer it had been. Sue Ellen was her friend, and you don't pray a friend's father away from her.

Suddenly, terribly, Mady was missing her own father. Not just thinking about him as she had earlier that day, but missing him with this terrible pinching pain. Her *father* . . .

She was glad that Sue Ellen and Mr. Forrest were going on talking. If she had a little while to be quiet, to sort of close in on herself, she could keep from crying. She steadied herself against the back of the cab and took deep breaths and tried to listen to what they said.

"What kind of a day did you have, Pop?" Sue Ellen was asking.

26

"Remarkable. Truly remarkable," said Mr. Forrest. He stopped for a light, turned, and looked at his passengers.

"I saved a man's life."

Chapter Three

Pop! What do you mean?" Sue Ellen gasped.

Mr. Forrest turned back to the traffic, drove on. "I didn't run over a guy," he said.

Sue Ellen burst out laughing. "Oh, *Pop*," she said reproachfully.

"I'm serious."

Sue Ellen was still giggling. "You haven't run over plenty of people just since we got in here. Did you save all their lives?"

"Some respect, young woman, please. I'll have you know that this cat jumped right in front of my hack.

I practically threw the brakes on the street, stopping in time, and slewed almost into the fence over there on Park Avenue."

"It was a cat?" Mady said, sitting up.

"No, no," said Mr. Forrest. "I meant a man. You know. Anyway, he almost demolished me so I could keep from demolishing him, if you see what I mean. So, I saved his life. He thought so, and I thought so. So it must've been a fact."

"What did you do? I mean *then*. Afterward," Sue Ellen asked breathlessly.

Mr. Forrest shrugged his heavy shoulders. "Drove him home. He lives in this big duplex on Park."

"Why did he walk in front of your cab?"

"Who knows? Thinking about something else, he said, and didn't watch the lights."

"He sounds sort of dumb."

"Oh, no. A nice guy. Well-spoken. Careless, you could say."

"My goodness, Pop," said Sue Ellen, wriggling happily. "You're a hero!" How impressed everyone was going to be! She could scarcely wait to get home. As the cab turned into their own street, she leaned forward, hand on the door handle, ready to escape and begin spreading the news.

"Now, look here," said Mr. Forrest, who could, both girls felt, read their minds. "Look here, Sue Ellen, Mady. I suppose I shouldn't have said anything about this at all, but it had just happened and

I *felt* like talking about it. But"—he fixed them, each in turn, with his brown, deep-seeing eyes—"I rely on you not to say anything to your friends. To anybody."

"Ah, gee, Pop."

"Not a word. If you'll think it over a bit, you'll see that you'd just be making a fool of me. Save a guy's life by not running over him, indeed."

"But you said—"

"Never mind what I said. Listen to what I'm saying."

"Okay," Sue Ellen said reluctantly.

"That's better. Now, run along."

"You mean we can't even tell Momma?"

Mr. Forrest rubbed the back of his neck, pushing his cap forward. "Me and my big mouth," he said. "I'll tell your mother. By this time it all sounds sort of ridiculous, doesn't it?"

"Not to me it doesn't—" Sue Ellen began, and was interrupted again.

"It does to me," said Mr. Forrest firmly. "So forget it, see?"

"Okay, Pop," Sue Ellen said again.

"Yes, Uncle Dan," said Mady, when he looked at her.

Mr. Forrest wasn't her uncle, not really. But she'd called him that for years. She called Mrs. Forrest Aunt Lillian. Her own real aunts and uncles lived in Alabama, and she hadn't seen them except so long ago that she'd forgotten. She had cousins too, down there. But here the Forrests were all the family she and her mother had.

Within herself Mady knew that she wouldn't trade the Forrests for a thousand real cousins and aunts and uncles. But she never said so to her mother, who wrote to the family in Alabama once in a while, and once in a while talked about Uncle Jack or Aunt Pam or Cousin Hank.

Mady had once asked her mother why they didn't go to visit these relatives, or why the relatives didn't come up here to visit. Momma had said the Alabama kin was too poor to come traipsing to New York City, and that she wouldn't go down there herself for a solid gold tiara.

"What's a tiara?" Mady had asked, forgetting about the relatives.

When they got out of the cab, Mr. Forrest said, "Tell your mother I'll be home as soon as I garage the hack. Won't be long. And you two stick around. I've got a surprise for you."

He drove off with a flip of his hand, and the two girls stood staring after him with love and pleasure. A surprise!

"What do you suppose . . . Now, just what can it be?" Sue Ellen wondered.

Mady couldn't answer, she felt so happy. A surprise.

They sat on the stoop to wait, watching the boys,

who had given up killing for stickball. They made as much noise, and fought more, playing games as they did when they were shooting. But anyway, they were occupied. If they hadn't been, Sue Ellen and Mady would have gone upstairs.

Boys, they had found, couldn't be idle without getting restless. When they got restless, they teased, and when they teased, after a while they tended to turn mean.

"They're funny, aren't they?" Mady said, watching them as they swung, hit, missed, ran, yelled, and shouted in triumph or disagreement.

"How do you mean?"

"Well, like you practically never see just one boy. Or even two boys, very much. They come in such bunches."

Mr. Forrest said the neighborhood they lived in was a racial stew. "Something of everything," he said. "White, colored, Oriental. Name it, we've got it."

But colored, Oriental, or white, in any mixture, to Mady's way of thinking, boys came in bunches.

"That's what makes them scary, I suppose," Sue Ellen said. She was not as fearful of them as Mady was, but Sue Ellen was not timid by nature. Still, she knew what Mady meant.

Girls, if they had nothing to do, could usually think of something to do, like a doll's tea party or a pretend shopping trip. Even, if they were restless or angry or unhappy, going someplace to cry. If boys were restless or angry or unhappy, they didn't go off by themselves. They got together and looked for someone to take it out on.

The best thing girls could do was stay out of their way.

Mrs. Forrest—when Sue Ellen had said something about the boys and how she and Mady wished they would all go away and live somewhere else, like maybe the North Pole, because then the neighborhood would be nice and peaceful—had shaken her head.

"No, no, *no*," she had said. "You mustn't talk like that. You must try to understand people, Sue Ellen. Not wish them out of your life, as if they had no right to exist. The boys around here, they're angry lots of the time—the way poor people get angry when they see all the things they can't have or do, when they think of all the things they can never be, just because they are poor. It's like a sore that won't heal. Like a huge unfairness that you can't do anything about. That's why they get so wild, sometimes. So destructive."

"Well, we're poor," Sue Ellen had said, not convinced. "And we don't get wild and destructive."

"We are not poor. We have a decent place to live and good food. We have love. Love's a kind of richness lots of those kids in the street never have. When you're without love and when you see all there is in the world that will never be for you, you get so you want to smash something, to show that you're *there*. To prove that you count."

"Why does smashing things or scaring people make anybody know you're there?"

Mrs. Forrest had shaken her head. "I don't know the *whys* of these things, lovey. I only know the *ares*. And smashing seems to work, somehow. At least somebody pays attention to you."

"Yeah, the cops."

"Maybe better than no attention at all," Mrs. Forrest had said, sounding tired.

Just the same, Mady and Sue Ellen were never allowed out at night. And at night even Mrs. Forrest locked her door.

It was all very hard to figure out. Lots of times their parents or the teachers said to them, "You'll understand when you're older." Mady and Sue Ellen figured it would have to wait until then, because right now they didn't understand any of it—the fear in the streets; the bolted doors; the roving gangs of older boys and girls, demanding attention from the police if from no one else.

Still, they weren't afraid in the daytime. Not if they were together and knew Mr. Forrest was going to come home soon.

"Hey, there he is!" said Sue Ellen, jumping up.

Mr. Forrest came strolling down the block, in his shirt-sleeves, carrying his jacket over one arm and a

34

package under the other. He grinned as Mady and Sue Ellen came dashing to meet him.

"Well, well," he said. "To what do I owe the pleasure of this salutation?"

"Just glad to see you, Pop."

Mady tried not to stare at the package, but her eyes kept going back to it.

"Is that the surprise?" Sue Ellen blurted.

"Mmm . . . might be. Now that you draw my attention to the matter, it is. Should have known all this ceremony wasn't for my beaux yeux."

"What's your bowz-yuh, Uncle Dan?" said Mady, impressed almost beyond bearing. It was French he was talking, she knew that much.

"My fine eyes," he explained, as they started upstairs. "My good looks, as it were."

"Well, it was for those," Mady said, but in such a whisper that neither Uncle Dan nor Sue Ellen, squabbling amiably over who was to carry the package, heard her.

Mrs. Forrest was getting dinner. She turned when they came in and said, "Did you remember that your mother is switching to the three to eleven shift today, Mady? You're to eat with us."

"Oh, no. I'd forgotten." Mady was ashamed of herself for feeling a rush of pleasure at these unexpected hours with the Forrests.

Mady loved her mother dearly, and she liked her too. What she couldn't do, lots of the time, was get along with her. Mrs. Guthrie worked very hard at the hospital and had, besides, to keep house and market and cook for Mady and herself. Mady tried to help sometimes, but the fact was—and she and her mother both knew it—she was more of a hindrance than a help. She was a slow-moving person, not like a salamander that way at all. Her mother was lively and quick as a squirrel. "Oh, darling, get *out* of the way," she'd say. "I can do this and six other things besides while you're making up your mind."

It was true, it was true. Many many times Mady had made up her mind to think fast, to act quickly, to do things *one, two, three, zip zap in a hurry*. It usually came out to something getting broken.

"Mady O'Grady's a dreamy lady . . ."

She heard it distantly, blinked, shook her head, and smiled at Uncle Dan.

"Mady O'Grady's *the* dreamiest lady," he chanted.

"Pop, what's the surprise?" Sue Ellen said, flicking an irritable glance in Mady's direction.

Mady pretended not to see. "Yes, what *is* it?" she said, trying to sound eager too, although Sue Ellen's expression had chilled her interest. "What is is *is* it?" she shrilled, and gave a little jump to emphasize her anticipation, because she didn't want to disappoint Uncle Dan.

36

"Oh, for Pete's sake," Sue Ellen said. "Do you have to be so dopey?"

Overwhelmed, Mady rushed from the apartment. With tears burning her face, blinding her eyes, she tried to push a key into the wrong lock. She fumbled, sniffled, her head tipped slightly backward, waiting for the footsteps, the approach she knew would come.

It was Aunt Lillian who walked across the hall, saying, "Mady—lovey—don't be upset. Sue Ellen's sorry she was cross. Come back, do."

Mady ran her hand across her nose and mouth, took a deep breath, and another. She couldn't talk yet.

"Here's some tissue," said Mrs. Forrest. "Blow your nose, and come to dinner. We're having meat loaf, your favorite."

"All right, Aunt Lillian. I'm sorry. I'm sorry I was dopey. Sometimes it—I don't know—"

"It takes you by surprise. Well, dopiness does that to all of us. And don't think all of us aren't dopes at one time or another."

"But with me it *shows* so," Mady wailed. She was, indeed, willing to believe that other people were as dumb and silly as she was sometimes, but never seemed to notice anyone but herself.

When she pointed this out, Mrs. Forrest said it was probably because she didn't notice much about

37

other people at all. "It's the way people are at your age," she said comfortingly, as if it were the right way for Mady to be. "You'll outgrow it."

"You're sure?"

"Perfectly sure."

Mr. Forrest and Sue Ellen were sitting on the sofa, the package still unopened between them.

"Come on," said Sue Ellen, patting the seat beside her. "We're *waiting.*"

Still sniffling a little, Mady smiled and went to stand in front of them.

"Here," said Sue Ellen, handing her the package. "Here, you open it."

It was a kite. A kite so beautiful that when Mr. Forrest had it assembled they all stood around, transfixed. Blue and red, with a wingspread of almost eighteen inches and a snaky white tail. It seemed to glow in the room.

"Like a bird out of a jungle," Mady breathed. "It's beautiful, Uncle Dan. Just heavenly beautiful."

"Shall we give it its first flying lesson? There's a good wind up, not too gusty." He looked at his wife. "Time before dinner?" he asked.

She laughed. "Could I say No?"

They filed out of the apartment after him, up the stairs to the roof, collecting a few neighbors on the way.

"These city buildings and the heat that's generated from them," Mr. Forrest explained, "make perfect air currents, like those in canyons out west. Perfect for the art of kite flying. You all understand, I trust, that it is an art. Takes skill, insight, hindsight, foresight, a delicate hand, a far-seeing eye, patience, judgment—" He broke off, frowning. "What happened to the wind?"

Sue Ellen stuck a finger in her mouth, held it up high. A slight coolness touched it on the fingernail side. "There's a wind, Pop. Put up your finger and see."

"When I came home the wind was making eddies of litter up and down the street. Practically a trash tornado. Now, just where did that wind go?" he demanded, looking at them sternly.

Sue Ellen and Mady giggled, as glances were exchanged all around. Some people couldn't tell with Mr. Forrest just when he was fooling. But they always could.

"Ah-hah! There it is!"

Everyone sprang to attention.

"Now," said Mr. Forrest, "observe that I stand with my back to this wind, the velocity of which I judge to be between ten and twelve miles an hour, with minor gusts. Releasing just a little of string, I wait until—ah, there we are, *there* we are—"

The kite fluttered, sprang up and down in Mr. Forrest's hand, tugged away from him, flew upward slightly, dipped down, started up again, as the watchers and the flyer held their breath and with the

very stance of their bodies tried to give buoyancy to the white-tailed red and blue bird.

One hand holding the stick around which the string was wound, the other holding the string itself —releasing it gently, a little at a time—Mr. Forrest talked—explaining, cajoling, praising the kite when it seemed about to take wing, reassuring it when it dived roofward again, all the time miraculously keeping it aloft.

A little more and a little more until at last, gloriously, the wind swooped beneath their kite and bore it skyward. When it was well up, sailing freely at the end of its long string, Mr. Forrest, just by turning his wrist, sent it into beautiful sweeps and dives, drawing it down a little then giving it its head so that it flew upward and away to hover far above them.

They stood with their heads thrown back, watching until their necks ached, then watching still. It was turning dark when at last, with an air of peaceful satisfaction, Mr. Forrest began to wind the string, to bring the kite home again out of the sky.

Chapter Four

When Mrs. Guthrie was working the three to eleven shift at the hospital, she got home a little before midnight. She always went into the kitchen to get herself a glass of milk before going to bed, and was very quiet.

Nevertheless, Mady always heard her. During the school year, except on weekends, she had to remain in bed so as not to disturb her rest. It was disturbed anyway as she pointed out to her mother, because once she woke up she was awake. But Mrs. Guthrie insisted that on school nights she must not get up.

Now, in July, she was free to get out of bed and

43

pad barefoot into the kitchen. It was to Mady an especially delicious time—quiet, with the clock ticking in its cross, silly little voice, and most of the buildings up and down the street darkened.

They did not put on the overhead light, but just a little lamp on the kitchen table, and they spoke in low voices. Mrs. Guthrie did not bother then to check around the apartment to see if it was in order, as she did when she got home in the afternoon.

There was something about this hour, about the stillness, the being awake when other people were sleeping, that Mady loved. It was cozy and secure. And it was different, something that everybody else wasn't doing. Even Sue Ellen was sleeping now, the same as the rest of the people. But Mady was awake, drinking milk, eating cookies, saying in a concerned tone, "How did you find Mr. Torrance today?"

"He's doing very well," said Mrs. Guthrie. "Better than could have been expected."

"That's good. Did his daughter come to see him yet?"

"No."

They sighed. Poor Mr. Torrance, old and sick and bad-humored, waiting for the sight of his daughter, who did not always find it convenient to visit him.

When Mrs. Guthrie had first begun to tell Mady about her patients, she'd explained that she mustn't use their names, as it would not be ethical. They'd tried using letters—Mr. T., Mrs. R.—but almost

44

without noticing, Mrs. Guthrie had slipped into the way of giving names. It was the only way they could keep track of which patient they were talking about.

They'd learned something from this, which was that Mady could keep a confidence. Never once, with anyone at all, had she repeated a word of these exchanges she and her mother had.

"You're such a comfort to me," Mrs. Guthrie said now. "Someone to talk to."

At this hour of the night Mady believed her. She felt like a comfort. In the afternoon when her mother got home from the seven to three shift, she might still say once in a while, "You're such a comfort," but a second later could add in the sharp, tart voice Mady knew well, "Is it absolutely necessary and required that you scatter your possessions around the place in this fashion? Is there a law to that effect?"

But now, in the glow of lamplight, munching Nabiscos, sipping cold milk, Mady inquired dreamily about Mrs. Schreiber, Mr. Katz, Miss Rowan.

Finally, reluctantly, she said, "Is Mrs. Carstairs better?"

"Mrs. Carstairs died early this evening," said her mother in a firm, blunt manner. Mrs. Guthrie did not believe in glossing over the truth and never said anyone had gone to heaven when she meant that they had died.

Mady's lip quivered. She'd never met Mrs. Car-

45

stairs or any of the other patients. But she knew them, cared about them. Even sour old Mr. Torrance had all her sympathy, although her mother said the daughter was entitled to some.

But Mrs. Carstairs—she hadn't been the least bit cross, though she'd been dying for a long, long time. So long, in fact, that Mady had begun to hope she never would. Anyway, not for years and years. Mrs. Carstairs had had a little body and a lively mind and Mady had known just what she looked like, just how she sounded. Like a grandmother. Like, Mady had said to herself but never to her mother, like *my* grandmama.

"A good, cheery, decent soul," Mrs. Guthrie said now. "But in bad pain toward the end. It was a deliverance."

Mady couldn't feel that to die was a deliverance. She shivered a little, and reminded herself that Mrs. Carstairs had been an old, old lady. It would be different, probably, if you were very, very old.

"We flew a kite today," she said, more loudly than she'd meant to. Lowering her voice, she went on, "Absolutely heavenly beautiful. Red and blue, with a white tail. It went up about eighty miles into the sky, sailing around and around. And before that, Uncle Dan gave us a ride in the taxi, from the ten-cent store—"

She broke off, as there came again that crunching

46

pain, that longing for her father she'd felt listening to Sue Ellen and Uncle Dan laughing together.

Her own father had died when she was only four years old. He had not been an old person like Mrs. Carstairs. He had been a young man, and he'd died for a cause. Mady knew how. But once in a while, like now, she wanted to hear again. Sometimes when she read a sad story in a book, she would read it over, hoping that this time it would turn out differently, this time the ending would be happy. She knew that her father's story, like the stories in the books, would never be different, would always have the same ending.

Just the same, every now and then she would say, "Momma, what did my Poppa die of?" She said it now.

Usually Mrs. Guthrie said, "He died in Mississippi of a gunshot wound." Tonight, when Mady had decided she was not going to answer at all, she said, "Of pride."

"How could somebody die of pride?"

"When pride becomes more important than life— or than your family—then you can die of pride, that's all."

"What was he proud of?"

"His people."

"Weren't we his people? You and me?"

"Yes. Only not just us. He used to say he saw

47

every child in you and every woman in me. He said he had to fight for all of us."

"Why did he have to fight for us in Mississippi? I mean, couldn't he have fought for us up here? Then he could have stayed here. And maybe not be—not be killed."

Mrs. Guthrie stared at the little lamp. "That's a question I've asked myself many a time, Mady. Only there's no one to answer it, is there? He was a man with a cause, and he went where it took him."

"I guess he loved the cause more than us," Mady said, and waited for her mother to tell her she was wrong.

It seemed to take a long time. Mrs. Guthrie looked blank, as if she'd forgotten what they were talking about. At last she said, "No. No, Mady. Your father loved you and me, very much. It's just—it's that some men have to fight for what they feel is right. No matter who gets hurt. No matter what the cost. It's how they are."

"But we're proud of him, aren't we?"

"Oh, yes. We're proud of him." Her mother's voice sounded so thin and sad that Mady wished she hadn't said that. It was only that once in a while she wanted to talk about her father.

"Was he handsome, Momma?"

"A very handsome man. A wonderful man. He laughed a lot, and loved animals. Like you, Mady.

48

Never could pass a stray dog or cat without patting it or getting it something to eat."

"Did he go to college, like Uncle Dan?"

As if she hadn't answered the question dozens of times before, Mrs. Guthrie said, "No. But he knew a lot. Your father knew a great deal about people and about life."

"Could he fly a kite?"

"He certainly could."

"I miss him," Mady whispered.

"Yes. So do I, Mady. We miss him." Mrs. Guthrie put her hand over her daughter's hand.

All at once Mady's eyelids were heavy, her voice drowsily muddled. She made no protest as her mother guided her back to bed, and she slept the moment she lay down.

In the morning she awakened early. Tiptoeing from the bedroom, clothes over her arm, she gently closed the bedroom door and crossed the living room to the kitchen. She closed that door too, and got herself some cornflakes and milk for breakfast. The glasses from the night before had been washed and put away, the crumbs all cleaned up.

I guess I never will be neat, Mady thought. She considered Aunt Lillian, who often had to wash the dishes just before dinner so as to have something to put the food on.

You'd think I was *their* child, she said to herself.

49

Forming the thought gave her a feeling of excitement, and of guilt. Suppose her mother could look into her head and *see* such a terrible idea!

Mady went out of the apartment, across the hall, and rang the Forrests' bell.

"My goodness, here you are already," said Mrs. Forrest when she answered.

Mady looked up at her quickly, but she was smiling, so that was all right.

"I came to see Sue Ellen."

"Did you now? Not to see me?"

"Oh, to see you too, you too," Mady said passionately, wrapping her arms around Mrs. Forrest's waist.

"My goodness," Aunt Lillian said again, patting Mady's head. "Well, Sue Ellen isn't awake yet, and I won't be the one to wake her."

"Me either," said Mady. She waited a moment. "Should I go back, Aunt Lillian?"

"No, no. Come in the kitchen with me. Would you like a doughnut and a cup of coffee?"

Reassured, utterly happy, Mady nodded.

Mrs. Forrest fixed a glass of warm milk with a tablespoon of coffee and a little sugar in it and set it before Mady. A delicious drink. The doughnut was powdery white with sugar. Sipping and munching happily, elbows on the table, Mady gazed around the kitchen.

Mr. Forrest's breakfast dishes were still on the

table, and a morning newspaper open to the sports section. Mixing bowls and pots weren't tidily stored away in closets but stood on the sideboard ready for instant use. The table where she sat was sugary and crumb-littered and besides the doughnut box and the newspaper there were an open cereal package, some jam jars, and a catsup bottle.

Mady's mother, who was devoted to her friend Lillian Forrest, said that the way the woman kept house was shocking. Mady loved it.

"Aunt Lillian?"

"Yes, lovey?"

"Wouldn't it be a terrible thing if people could see into other people's heads? I mean, look right in and see what they were thinking?"

"Oh, now, you don't have such dreadful thoughts as all that, I'm sure. If I looked into your head right now, for instance, what would I see?"

Mady straightened, surprised and upset. She had not expected Aunt Lillian to ask her that.

"Well, but Aunt Lillian," she said in confusion, "I couldn't *tell* you something like that. I mean, I was just saying it was a good thing people *couldn't* look and see. What I was thinking was, there is your forehead, with all that thinking in back of it, and your forehead is like a wall, you know, that nobody can look through."

"Sometimes people can guess."

"I suppose so," Mady said slowly. "But they

51

couldn't ever be sure, could they? No matter what they guessed. They couldn't be sure unless they could look right *at* a thought."

"This is certainly mysterious. Perhaps you'd better tell me what you are thinking, Mady."

"Oh, no. I mean—I'm not thinking anything at all. Only *thinking* about thinking about—" She stopped, closing her lips tight. She supposed she wasn't making herself clear, because Aunt Lillian didn't seem to understand what she was trying to say.

Still—she went on with the idea in silence—still it was a *very* good thing that foreheads were there, and not see-throughable. Because right now, if Aunt Lillian could look in her head, she'd see that Mady was thinking how she didn't understand things. And she'd see too, maybe, that thought about wishing she was their daughter and not her own mother's.

One look at *that,* and Aunt Lillian would start scolding for sure.

"Is Uncle Dan going to fly the kite for us again today?" she asked. "When he gets home?"

"Shouldn't be surprised. What do you and Sue Ellen have planned for today?"

"I don't know. Just have a little day, I suppose."

"A little day?"

"You know. Not do much. Sue Ellen said yesterday that maybe we'd sew some clothes for our dolls."

They had a box where they kept scraps of material. Most of it was just sort of old stuff, clean because Mady's mother washed and ironed their scraps, but faded and thinnish. However, among the scraps, here and there, once in a while, they had pieces of perfectly lovely material. Only last week Mrs. Guthrie had brought home nearly half a yard of dark blue nylon velvet and a square of green silk threaded with gold. A patient had given them to her after hearing about the scrap box. Mady wanted to make her dancing doll, Vera, something from the green silk, and Sue Ellen planned to use some of the velvet to make Geneva an evening dress.

"She needs something elegant, just once in her life," Sue Ellen had said. "So she won't think she's *only* a rag doll."

"If we could take the subway by ourselves," Mady said now to Mrs. Forrest, "we could go to the zoo in Central Park. They have a place with baby animals in it and—"

"Now, Mady. You know you can't do that. Not until you're older."

"Well, but when will we be able to?"

"I don't know. When you're fourteen, or thirteen, maybe."

She could as well have said forty for all the comfort that offered Mady. "Aunt Lillian, maybe *you* could take us—"

53

"No, lovey. I'm going to be busy all day. Some other time, perhaps."

Busy doing what? Mady wondered, and again was thankful that no one could read her mind. At the same time she wished she'd stop thinking about that. It was a way she had. She'd get a notion, and then it would stay and stay with her, and the harder she tried not to think it, the more she thought it.

Probably, she said to herself with resignation, I'll go all *day* thinking about how nobody can see what I'm thinking.

Just the same, she'd bet a cookie Aunt Lillian didn't have much to do except poke around and visit with Mrs. Gerez or somebody. Mrs. Guthrie had said once that Lillian Forrest was the world's principal darling, but was lazy as all get-out.

Mady had flared up. "She is not either," she'd said hotly. "She's not either lazy."

Mrs. Guthrie, looking at her fingernails, had replied, "I'm sorry, Mady. I shouldn't have said that. She's wonderful to you, to both of us." She'd added softly, a little bitterly, "It's important to be grateful. Anyway, she *is* splendid, and it was wrong of me to speak that way," she'd concluded in a warm, honest voice.

Mady had wanted to grumble some more, but you couldn't stay angry with somebody who apologized for what they said.

She looked at Aunt Lillian now and thought daringly, safely hidden behind her forehead, "You're lazy as all get-out. You never take us anywhere." And then, because it was true and far more important, she added, "I love you, Aunt Lillian. You're wonderful."

Chapter Five

The day, as Mady had predicted, remained little.

Mrs. Guthrie came over to the Forrests even before Sue Ellen got up and said she needed Mady to help her.

"Have some coffee and a doughnut first," said Mrs. Forrest. "No need to rush."

For a moment Mrs. Guthrie seemed about to contest that, but she sat down, refusing the doughnut, taking her coffee black.

"How do you do it?" said Mrs. Forrest, looking from her neighbor's slender figure to her own ample one. "How can you keep from eating all the time? I declare, I'm hungry just about all the time." She did not sound especially regretful. "How's work, Anna?"

"Interesting. Tiring. Lots of it. We're short-handed, as always. Never seem to catch up, never do as much as we should. Or want to."

"When are you going to get some time off?"

"At this rate, not till fall."

"But Momma!" Mady protested. "I'll be back in school then. You said on your vacation we could go to Bear Mountain or something. We could have a picnic. You said you'd take Sue Ellen and me to the Bronx Zoo! But if you don't get *any* time off, we can't do anything! It isn't fair—"

"Mady, stop pestering," said Mrs. Forrest. "Your momma feels as badly about it as you do, I'm sure. Worse, probably."

Mady didn't see how she could feel worse. The whole summer was going to go by and she and Sue Ellen would never get anywhere but the ten-cent store. It wasn't fair.

She lapsed into scowling silence while the two women had their coffee and talked about the war and the President and the terrible ways in which people suffered and were humiliated and given promises that were always broken. They didn't exactly say Negro people, and Mady knew that white people suffered from those things too. What you had to do to suffer and get humiliated and have promises

57

to you broken—what you had to do was be poor. Without asking or being told, Mady sensed that there were more poor Negroes than white people. In a way she didn't like it when the Forrests and Momma talked about these things, and in another it fascinated her. Sometimes she thought that besides leaving her a deep love for animals, her father had left her his feeling for the cause. She wasn't old enough to be sure yet, and was a long way from being able to do anything about it. But some day, some day she would.

She realized, all at once, that Momma and Aunt Lillian were talking about a husband for Mrs. Guthrie. She could tell because they looked at her sharply, as if to be sure she wasn't listening. She kept her eyes vague, her features vacant, as if she were dreaming.

Even then they skirted all around because of "little pitcher with big ears." They could never be sure when the little pitcher was all ears, even if it didn't appear to be.

So Mrs. Forrest said, "Anything stirring on the—ah, the—marital front?"

Mady smiled inwardly. They thought the word marital would be beyond her. The truth was, there were very few words they used between them that were beyond Sue Ellen and Mady. But she stared at the floor with an absent-minded scowl and they felt safe.

"How could anything stir?" said Anna Guthrie. "Where are the candidates?"

"Oh, there must be some, in your line of work."

"Sick people?"

"Relatives. Visiting relatives. Or—your colleagues. MD's, you know. That would be ideal."

Aunt Lillian wants Momma to marry a doctor, Mady translated. She would have liked that herself. Doctors were smart and gentle and if her mother married one, she wouldn't have to work anymore. Or they could move to the suburbs and have an office in their house and Momma could be the office nurse.

She dreamed away briefly and lost some of their conversation.

"Come on, Mady," she heard her mother saying impatiently. "Come along. We have things to do."

"Oh, don't go yet," said Aunt Lillian.

But Mady rose. She knew her mother's firmness.

"We have to go down to the Laundromat and the market," said Mrs. Guthrie. "And then I have an ironing to do, and some cooking. And Mady's to clean the bathroom and kitchen."

"They're clean already," Mady offered.

"Not as clean as they're going to be. Is there anything we can do for you, Lil?"

Mrs. Forrest felt that they could get her a few little things at the market. "Save me steps," she said comfortably. "Can't thank you enough."

"The shoe is on the other foot," said Mrs.
Guthrie, looking at Mady. "I don't know what we'd
do, if it weren't for you."

"Now, now. I love her like my own, you know
that."

Feeling warm and cherished, no longer minding
the chores ahead, Mady went with her mother.

"Tell Sue Ellen I'll be back," she called over her
shoulder.

"I'll do that."

She didn't get back until after lunch. She and her mother, when the marketing and laundry were attended to, worked around the apartment until lunchtime, and then it was time for Mrs. Guthrie to get dressed for work. Mady waited, to see her in her white uniform.

Somehow she never got tired of looking at and admiring her mother, dressed for the hospital. Crisp and trim and pretty in her white dress with the little gold pin on her pocket, wearing white shoes and stockings, carrying her starched nurse's cap in a bag, she looked at Mady and smiled sweetly.

"How do I look, darling?"

"Any man would want to marry you, Momma. You're beautiful!"

Mrs. Guthrie looked startled, then threw back her head and laughed. It was such a gay and sudden sound that Mady, in a moment, laughed too.

"There's no hiding anything from you, is there?" said Mrs. Guthrie, putting an arm around Mady's shoulder. "You're *too* smart."

"But Momma," Mady said seriously, "I think you should get married."

"Well, perhaps I shall, one day. Have to dash now. See you tonight, except don't get up unless you want to."

"You know I want to," Mady said, but her mother had already gone, running lightly down the stairs.

61

Mady leaned on the windowsill, watching her go up the street. At the corner, she turned and waved. Momma never just walked away from a person. She always turned that way, and waved. To show that you were still in her mind, that she hadn't already started thinking about the next thing.

Her mother hardly ever laughed right out loud, the way she had a little bit ago. But she also never complained. "We're lucky," she'd say whenever Mady tried even a little complaint. "We are very, very lucky, and you mustn't forget it. If you could see what I see—what people have to put up with, what they do without. The old ones, the children, the people waiting all day in the clinics, waiting and waiting for someone to care at *all* about what happens to them. No, don't grumble to me, Mady. I have no patience with it."

Mady once had tried to say that complaining, like about how she'd probably *never* get to a zoo, made her feel better. But Momma had hardly let her finish the sentence.

She stood now, looking around. This was a nice apartment. Her mother had made new slipcovers last winter. Zebra-striped, with red cushions thrown on the sofa and one chair. There were white curtains at the window, and a cherry-colored rug on the floor. It was nicer than any other apartment in the building.

There were in the world, of course, places far grander than this apartment where she and her mother lived. Mady knew that from the movies and television. There were places you couldn't even believe that people lived in.

But this is a nice, pretty apartment, Mady thought happily. And Momma's right, I guess. We shouldn't complain.

She got Mrs. Forrest's groceries and went across the hall to her friends.

Sue Ellen had a box of beads, all sorts of beads. Lots of them belonged to Mady, but they kept them together like a treasure trove in a little chest Mr. Forrest had made. Today Sue Ellen had decided they could string beads.

"But what about the dolls?" Mady asked. "We were going to sew for them."

"They've waited this long, they can wait a little longer. Unless," Sue Ellen added coolly, "you'd *rather* sew than string all these beautiful beads."

"But I wasn't the one—" Mady began.

"I got a marvelous string of pink beads from Mrs. Gerez," Sue Ellen interrupted. "All different colors of pink. Enormous beads. Do you want to see?"

Well, it wouldn't hurt the dolls to wait.

They strung beads. It was one of the best things to do. Getting your needle and the thick thread ready, putting a little bead at the end and knotting it tight to keep the next beads from slipping off, then putting your hand into the treasure trove, stirring it carefully, leaning over to select a round pink bead, a diamond one, a green one shaped like a tiny egg with cut sides, a few pearls, another round pink one . . .

A nice day, but a little one, right up until evening. They'd had dinner and Mr. Forrest was finishing up his morning paper, doing the crossword puzzle, when the day exploded into bigness.

Chapter Six

A five-letter word for cour-
teous," Mr. Forrest was saying. "Let's see . . . fifth
letter, *l*. Ah . . . *civil*. Which makes seventeen
down *vortex,* and—"

The doorbell rang.

"See who it is, will you, lovey?" said Mrs. Forrest
to her daughter, unnecessarily, as Sue Ellen was
already on her way.

"It's a man, Momma," said Sue Ellen, making it
clear that it was not a man they knew. Mr. and Mrs.
Forrest got to their feet as the stranger entered.

Mady, who'd been reading *In Which Piglet Meets*

a Heffalump for maybe the fifteenth time and enjoying it as much as ever, went on reading for a moment, but looked up with sudden attention at Uncle Dan's tone.

"Well, I'll be—" said Uncle Dan. "It's you. How did you find me? I mean, what're you here for? Excuse me, that doesn't sound very hospitable. I'm surprised, that's all."

The man came in and sat down at Mrs. Forrest's gesture toward a chair.

Mady and Sue Ellen looked at him with devouring curiosity. A white man. And he didn't look as if he came from around here. There were lots of white people living in the neighborhood, as well as black people and in-between people. But this was a poor neighborhood, and this man was not dressed poorly. Not like a teacher or a social worker, either.

Mady decided he looked like a man in an advertisement telling you which bank to get your auto loan at.

"This is Mr. Kusack, Lillian," said Uncle Dan. "My wife, Mr. Kusack."

The stranger rose, shook hands with Mrs. Forrest, and looked at Sue Ellen and Mady.

"And are these your little girls?"

"Yes," said Uncle Dan. He added thoughtfully, "We think of them that way. Sue Ellen there is a Forrest, and Mady O'Grady—I mean, Mady Guthrie—is our good friend."

"I see, I see," Mr. Kusack said, and sat down again. He said, "Thank you, that would be nice," when Mrs. Forrest offered him a cup of coffee. "Did your husband tell you about me?" he asked her.

"No," said Mrs. Forrest in a baffled way. "I don't think so."

"Sure I did, Lil. This is the man I almost hit with the hack yesterday. I hope you're feeling all right now, Mr. Kusack."

Uncle Dan was looking at the man suspiciously, and the two girls could tell from Mrs. Forrest's voice as she offered cream and sugar that she was uneasy. Even nervous. That made them nervous.

"Is something wrong?" Mrs. Forrest asked cautiously.

"Why, no. Nothing's wrong at all," said the man, putting his coffee on the table beside him, rubbing the tip of his nose with his index finger. "Far from it." He glanced at Sue Ellen and Mady, hesitated, looked at Mr. Forrest.

"Girls," said Uncle Dan, "run along over to Mady's for a little while, okay?"

"But, Pop—"

"Scat."

They went, whispering furiously. In the hall Sue Ellen suggested that they put their ears against the door and listen, but somebody was coming upstairs, so they had to go to Mady's after all.

"If he's coming to make trouble for Pop, I'll—"

Sue Ellen couldn't think of what she could do that would be bad enough and still not sound violent. Her parents did not hold with violence.

"Why should he make trouble? After all, your father saved his life, remember?"

"Maybe he doesn't see it that way," Sue Ellen said grimly. "Some people go around suing other people all the time."

"What for? What could he sue him for?"

"For almost hitting him, maybe," said Sue Ellen, close to tears. "For—anything he wanted to make up, that's what for."

"But your father doesn't have any money that people could sue away from him. Besides, that man is rich."

"How do you know that?"

"I just do," Mady said vaguely. "He walks rich."

"Well, rich people are the worst of all. They don't care what happens to *any*body, just so they get some more money."

Mady didn't know anything about that and didn't think Sue Ellen did either. She repeated, "Uncle Dan doesn't have any money, does he?"

"No, you dope. Of course he doesn't. But the company does, and the man could sue the company and Pop could lose his job. Oh, I *hate* that Mr. Kusack. I wish he'd get eaten by rats. I wish Pop *had* hit him with the taxi." She stopped, folding her lips, to keep from saying anything violent.

Mady found that she was trembling. "Don't call me a dope."

"I'll call you anything I want to. Oh, Mady!" Sue Ellen wailed, breaking down. "What are we going to do?"

"Now, don't *worry*," Mady said loudly. "Don't worry, you hear me? Uncle Dan knows—he knows how to handle things. Everything'll be fine. You'll see."

It seemed an hour before Mrs. Forrest came over and knocked and said they could come back. Mr. Kusack was no longer there.

"Pop!" cried Sue Ellen, bursting into the living room ahead of her mother and Mady. "What'd that buzzard want? I'll slit his gizzard, that's what I'll do!"

"Now, Sue Ellen," Mrs. Forrest remonstrated mildly.

"Oh, the buzzard and the lizard left their gizzard in the blizzard and who should come and find it but a very hungry wizard—"

Mr. Forrest hummed and grinned, and the two girls relaxed. It was all right, then. Everything was all right.

"Well, but what *did* he want?" Sue Ellen asked.

"Wanted to thank me."

"He thanked you yesterday, you said."

"Wanted to reward me."

"With money, Pop?" Sue Ellen asked curiously.

69

"That was his original intent. A nice enough fellow, but not very sensitive. Or maybe it's just that people with a lot of money get to thinking money is the whole bag. That's a possibility."

"What'd you say to him?"

"Told him I didn't take cash for not running down pedestrians. Told him I'd be a rich man too, if that was a path to riches."

"I'll bet that put his hat on straight," Sue Ellen said admiringly.

"He was embarrassed. Still, the upshot is, I got rewarded after all. That is, if it's agreeable to you two."

Sue Ellen and Mady exchanged glances.

"Us?"

"Just so. This fellow, this Kusack, among his other interests has part interest in a summer camp for girls. How do you like that for a summer treat?"

Sue Ellen's mouth fell open, and Mady felt her pulse begin to throb.

Camp? The country? Trees and wild animals and sleeping under the stars? For me? For us, me and Sue Ellen? Mady couldn't speak, for fear of being wrong.

"What do you say?" Mr. Forrest asked, looking at them intently. "Would you like to go to camp for a couple of weeks, or even a month? Mr. Kusack says he can get you in even this late in the season. A couple of girls, daughters of a friend of his, backed out at the last minute, just last night. So there are

70

two openings, and Kusack suggests you two might want to go instead. You'd have to leave Wednesday."

Sue Ellen swallowed hard. "You mean—the day after tomorrow?"

"That's it."

All this time Mrs. Forrest hadn't spoken, but now she said, "It's entirely up to you, of course, girls. Don't feel you *have* to accept just because it was offered."

Sue Ellen shook her head slowly from side to side. "I don't want to. I don't want to go to the country with a lot of strangers and—are they all white at this camp?"

"Nope. Mr. Kusack says it's a satisfactory mixture."

"I don't care. I won't go."

Mr. Forrest transferred his glance to Mady. "Well, Miss Silence? What do you say?"

Bitterly disappointed, so angry at Sue Ellen she could not bring herself to look at her, Mady answered sullenly, "What's to say? It's all been said, hasn't it?"

"I don't look at it that way," Mr. Forrest answered. "The invitation is for either or both. If you'd like to go, Mady, give the word. We'd have to get you a few things. Sleeping bag, for one. Kusack says they don't wear a uniform up there, just shorts and the sort of thing you have. Have to take your own bed linen—"

Sue Ellen was looking at Mady in astonishment.

71

"You mean, you're going to go? All by yourself? Are you crazy?"

Mady, who'd been about to tell Uncle Dan that she couldn't, not possibly, go by herself, go somewhere without Sue Ellen, set her jaw.

"I want to," she said. There was a tremor in her voice despite her determination, and Sue Ellen pounced.

"There," she said. "You're scared already and won't admit it. I bet if you went, you'd be home the next day. I bet—"

"Stop that!" Mrs. Forrest said sharply. "I'm ashamed of you, Sue Ellen. Truly ashamed. If you don't want to go, fine and good. But to frighten Mady—"

"I don't have to frighten her. She's already frightened."

"I am *not*. And you don't frighten me, either." Mady looked at Uncle Dan and Aunt Lillian. "I guess it is sort of—funny. Funny peculiar, not funny ha-ha. Besides, I have to ask Momma. But she'll say Yes. She'll be glad, I bet."

Whether she meant that her mother would be glad for her to have a camping time or glad just to be alone for a while, she didn't know. I don't care, either, she thought. Just now she didn't care what Momma or Sue Ellen or anybody else thought.

To go to camp! To be, her very self, Mady Guthrie, in the country with the grass and flowers

72

and animals. A lake. There'd have to be a lake at a camp, wouldn't there? And Uncle Dan had said a sleeping bag, so that meant she *would* get to sleep out-of-doors, under the stars.

And maybe hear an owl.

All her life she'd wanted to hear an owl hoot. All her life she'd thought what it would be like to lie out-of-doors, under the trees and the sky, with maybe a raccoon walking up to lick her face. She wouldn't be afraid—not of any animal, not of the dark, not of anything.

There'd be all those strange girls. A campful of strangers, and her, Mady, all by herself. Almost, she wavered. Just for a moment her resolution flickered. Would it be worth it? To have the grass and the animals and the lake and the sleeping out, but also all those strange people and no Sue Ellen to protect her?

No, no, no! She didn't mean *protect*. She didn't need Sue Ellen's protection. She just meant it would be funny to be somewhere without Sue Ellen. They'd practically started out in the same cradle.

But Sue Ellen, she thought, said No without even asking how I felt. She always thinks she's saying Yes or No for both of us about everything.

"I don't care," she said aloud. "I want to go."

"Then it's settled," said Mr. Forrest. "If your mother agrees, of course. She'll be glad for you to have this experience. Now, where can we get a sleeping bag? Army-Navy store, I'd say, wouldn't you? And a duffel bag to put your stuff in. That should do it."

"She'll need a bathing suit," said Mrs. Forrest. "And I'd better check over her socks and shorts. She may need a few more of those. Perhaps a couple of wash and wear shirts. And, let's see—"

At every item Mady's heart sank further. "It's too much," she whispered. "Momma can't afford all that. I can't—oh, I can't *go*, Uncle Dan! Momma can't ever—"

"Now, now," said Aunt Lillian calmly. "Don't fret so, Mady. Lots of this stuff we can get at the Thrift Shop. Besides, your Momma's making a little extra working nights. We'll work it out somehow, never you fear."

"Well, I think you're all crazy, that's what I think," said Sue Ellen loudly. "And you know what else I think? I think you're taking charity, that's what you're doing. Just plain taking—"

"That will be enough!"

Even Mady, absorbed in her own dilemma— wanting and not wanting, longing and trembling— was shocked at Mr. Forrest's tone. She'd never heard him so severe, so angry.

"Is it charity," Mr. Forrest asked his daughter, "when someone invites you someplace and you accept? Charity if a person wins a scholarship and accepts that? Is it charity when somebody takes a

74

challenge, as Mady is doing? I won't hear anything more from you, young lady, about charity."

Sue Ellen drew a deep breath. Her cheeks were hot, her stomach sort of cold. She'd gone too far, and she knew it and did not know how to get back.

It was Mady's fault too. What did she think she was doing, going off someplace nobody knew anything about to be among strangers who'd probably be horrible to her?

They had the whole summer ahead of them, practically, to do all the things they always did together. Sewing for the dolls, having tea parties, going to the ten-cent store, playing in the hydrant. Probably sometime they'd even be able to talk Pop into taking them to the Bronx Zoo. And now Mady was spoiling it all.

She's ungrateful, that's what she is, Sue Ellen thought wildly. Ungrateful, horrible girl. And after all we've done for her! Her mouth opened, snapped shut. If she said *that*, she'd be in the worst mess of her life. She stared at her father and mother, almost afraid that she had said it.

For the first time Sue Ellen was aware of what *saying* something could do to a person's life. Right now, at this very second, she might already have spoken those words. *After all we've done for her!* And once they'd been said aloud, it would be too late ever to get them back. There'd be no way ever in the world to make out that she hadn't said them.

Mady, who was timid but was proud, probably never would speak to her again. And her mother and father! Their disappointment in her, their sadness, would have been too awful to bear.

She felt weak and so relieved at having for once, and at such an important time, kept her mouth shut that she babbled an apology. "I'm sorry, honestly, everybody. I didn't mean it, really and truly I didn't—"

Her mother patted her hand. "It's an exciting time. I guess we're all a bit jumpy at the whole idea. And of course you'll miss Mady. We all will. Sometimes, when we're unhappy, we just snap at people without thinking."

They're so good, my mother and father, Sue Ellen thought. They were the best and kindest people she'd ever known, and if she lived forever, she'd never be that good herself.

A secret voice within her said, "I wouldn't want to be that good," and this time Sue Ellen wasn't afraid she would accidentally speak out loud. Because that was a thing she'd been saying to herself, secretly, for a long time. She adored her mother and father, but she didn't want to be like them. Not completely. And anyway, if she had wanted to, she couldn't. Because she had perfectly terrible thoughts and wishes sometimes. Unkind, violent, angry—all the things her parents didn't hold with.

Just the same she wasn't going to stay here and let

Mady go off to the country. Maybe I'd miss her and maybe I wouldn't, Sue Ellen said to herself. But if mousy Mady Guthrie can take herself off to camp, then so can I.

"When you call Mr. Kusack," she said coldly, "you can tell him there'll be two of us getting the treat."

Chapter Seven

Mrs. Guthrie was
to take them to Grand Central Station on Wednesday morning. Mr. Forrest said he couldn't get
the day off, and Mrs. Forrest announced that she
would be sure to cry and disgrace everybody.

"Oh, Momma!" Sue Ellen moaned, looking ready
to cry herself. "Momma, it's awful!"

Wednesday morning came. The two duffel bags
and two sleeping bags, with name tags attached,
were by the door. The prospective campers sat on
kitchen chairs, the one looking grim, the other

dreamily distant, and the three adults sat with them.

No one had been able to eat much, and conversation had gone in little runs, stops, jerks, and gasps. Sue Ellen went into the bathroom once, sure she was going to be sick. But she wasn't, and after a while she came back saying, "Anyway . . . anyway, it's only for two weeks."

Mady said nothing. Perhaps she hadn't even heard.

They had told Mr. Kusack when they telephoned him that everyone was grateful for the opportunity, very happy. "But we feel two weeks will be ample, just fine," Mr. Forrest had said. He hadn't added that everyone except Mady had decided two weeks were all they wished to accept. "No, really, Mr. Kusack," they'd heard him say firmly. "Our girls have never been away from us before, and we all feel . . . yes, yes, that's it. I'm glad you understand." There'd been some more talk, but finally Mr. Forrest had hung up and, as Sue Ellen had put it to herself, it was too late now to back out.

At Grand Central they went nervously into the big waiting room, where they'd been told a sign for the camp would be readily visible. It was.

CAMP ORIOLE, printed in red. There was no missing it. A crowd of girls milled about. Two counselors, a man and woman, were greeting campers and parents. Mady and Sue Ellen, clutching their lunch boxes which they'd been told to bring because the train ride to Vermont was so long, stared around.

Sue Ellen's eyes were glazed. She grabbed Mrs. Guthrie's hand. "Let me *out*," she said hoarsely. "I've changed my mind, I tell you!"

But with all the noise there was in this place, nobody heard her. Before she could say it again, louder, Mrs. Guthrie had taken them both up to the counselors.

"I'm Mrs. Guthrie," she said. "I have my—I have Sue Ellen Forrest and Mady Guthrie here. I mean, you do know about them?"

Oh, crimers, thought Sue Ellen. Suppose old Kusack never even mentioned us? Her face felt hot, and the palms of her hands were wet. She tried to wipe them on her skirt without seeming to . . . just put her hands lightly on her hips and pushed down.

Still, if kooky Kusack *hadn't* mentioned them to these counselors, she thought, brightening, they could forget the whole mess and go home.

Mady hadn't said a word. She never did talk much, of course, but it seemed to Sue Ellen that she hadn't opened her mouth since Monday night. Just gone around with that sappy faraway look.

But this was awful. Absolutely awful. And they hadn't even got started with the camping part. Hadn't got out of the city yet. How was she going to stand two weeks of this?

"Surest thing you know," said the man counselor, shoving his hand at Mrs. Guthrie. "I'm Bob Franks. And this is Miss Burdoski." He looked down at Sue Ellen and Mady. "Which of you is which?"

"I'm Mady Guthrie," Mady said, looking up at the two counselors with serene confidence.

"Then you'll be Sue Ellen, right?" said Mr. Franks.

"You sure worked that one out," said Sue Ellen. She heard Mrs. Guthrie's little *thhu* of annoyance and felt Mady's glare, but continued to eye the two counselors. They weren't going to get her down or pull a pal act on her.

"Welcome to Camp Oriole," said the lady counselor. She was white, but awfully tan. Mr. Franks was colored, but awfully light. Sue Ellen noticed—she'd often noticed this exact same thing—that it came out to practically the same color. Oh, well. She shrugged, looked icily around, and sat down on her duffel bag.

In a few moments Mr. Franks said, "We'll be starting now. If you'll all line up, two by two, and go past me—but not too fast, friends—I can check you off and we'll go over to our train."

He held his clipboard and pencil at the ready, and the kids all began to say good-bye to their parents. There was a lot of hugging and kissing and some crying. Mrs. Guthrie kissed Mady, then looked at

Sue Ellen, who got up resignedly and allowed herself to be kissed too.

Then she and Mady were alone with this bunch of strangers.

As they walked across the great station plaza Mady felt all the people looking at them.

"I bet they wonder what we're doing," she whispered to Sue Ellen.

"Yeah? Well, so do I."

"Oh, Sue Ellen, don't be crabby. Let's have fun, *please?*"

"Go ahead and have fun. I'm not stopping you."

"I can't have fun if you don't."

"I don't like marching in the middle of summer. I feel like I was back in school or had joined the Army or something."

Mady giggled, and that made Sue Ellen feel a little better. She smiled briefly, shifted her duffel bag, and said to herself, *What the heck. Two weeks. I can make it.*

They got a seat together on the train and did not, like a lot of the other campers, run up and down the aisle, or throw another seat back so that four could sit face to face, or crowd around the counselors asking questions and yelling things about last year.

"You suppose they've all been there before?" Mady asked edgily.

"Nah. Some of them, I guess."

"But they all seem to know each other. They're all talking."

"Well, so are we talking. I bet if you looked, you'd see plenty of kids sitting all by themselves with *nobody* to talk to. We're lucky."

But neither of them wanted to look around. They sat staring at the back of the seat in front of them as the train ran out of the city.

"It's my mother's birthday next Monday," Sue Ellen said after a long silence.

Mady gasped. "I forgot! How *could* I? Maybe I can send a card from the camp, Sue Ellen. I'll make her a present, maybe, in that arts and crafts shop Mr. Kusack said they have at Camp Oriole."

Sue Ellen was gratified that Mady had forgotten, but she wasn't going to show it. She said casually, "I left her something. A surprise."

"You did? What? Anyway, it won't be a surprise if—"

"Yes, it will," Sue Ellen interrupted. "I gave Pop a note to give her on Monday morning, and she's going on a treasure hunt to find my present."

She turned eagerly to Mady, who was looking at her, open-mouthed. "In my note I tell her to go to the kitchen cabinet and look behind the flour jar. A note back of that tells her to walk five paces to the sugar canister, and underneath that is a note telling her to go in the living room and look under the edge of the rug, and that note tells her to go in the

84

bedroom and look under her bed and there she'll find a *great surprise!*"

Mady said enviously, "What a neat idea, Sue Ellen. I wish I'd thought to leave something for my momma."

"It isn't her birthday."

"No, but just the same. I wish I'd left her a note or something. She would have liked that." Preoccupied with regret, she didn't ask Sue Ellen what the great surprise was going to be, but Sue Ellen told her anyway.

"I made her a cookbook."

"Oh, Sue *Ellen!* Oh, how marvelous. How super-*scrump*tious. How did you *do* it?"

Sue Ellen, more and more pleased, said, "Well, I went to the library, see, and got out a whole lot of cookbooks, and then I copied some of the recipes into this little notebook I bought. Easy recipes," she confessed. "Without too much writing in them. Anyway, Momma only likes to cook easy things. I drew pictures in it too. A fish carrying a fork, and a chicken with a mushroom for an umbrella." She sighed with satisfaction and then with discontent. "I wish I could see her when she gets it. I wish the whole stupid treat was over and this train was going in the other direction."

Mady didn't reply. With the long morning, and the train that was so dirty and dismal, and the way those two counselors just sat with the other kids, talking and laughing, she was beginning to come around to Sue Ellen's point of view about this treat they were getting.

"Maybe," she whispered, "we could write to your pop and tell him we changed our minds."

"Changed our minds?"

"Tell him we want to go home."

"Say hey, Mady. That's a great idea! If I had some paper, I'd start the letter right now." She looked toward the counselors. "Suppose he'd let me have a piece of paper from his clipboard?"

Mady, feeling rushed, said, "No, no. Don't ask him. That would be—it wouldn't be polite. Anyway, Sue Ellen, I only said *maybe*. I mean, suppose we love it?"

"Fat chance."

But Mady wasn't entirely prepared to give up, yet. She was going to the country, where she had never been before, and even if she was lonesome, even if she was sort of frightened, she didn't want to be talked into leaving before she'd seen it. She wished she'd kept still, because once Sue Ellen got an idea, she hung on like a rat.

After a while all the children got out their lunches, and the counselors opened a big plastic carryall they had with them and handed around little cartons of milk.

"How's it going with you two?" said Bob Franks, perching on the arm of Mady's seat.

"Oh, everything's neat," said Mady eagerly, bouncing a little in the pleasure of being noticed. Sue Ellen stared out the window. Or at it. It was hard to see through the grime.

"How about you, Sue Ellen?" Mr. Franks persisted.

Impressed that he remembered her name, out of so many kids, she turned toward him and said slowly, "Okay, I guess. I mean, when we get there—"

"Sure, sure," he said, laughing lightly. "This train isn't exactly heaven on wheels, is it?"

"Oh, it's *nice*," Mady said. "Honestly, Mr. Franks. It's peachy."

Sue Ellen gave her a disgusted look, but Mady refused to be quelled. She wouldn't even look at Sue Ellen but kept on staring up at Mr. Franks.

"Call me Bob, girls. All the counselors are called by their first names. We like it better that way."

Hah-*hah,* said Sue Ellen to herself.

"What's her—What's Miss—ah—" Mady began.

"Burdoski. That's a tough one, isn't it? Her name is Maria, and she'll be along to talk to you before the trip is over. We like to get to know everyone during this ride."

Mady started to ask him what it was going to be like when they were at camp. She wanted to ask what it would look like, where they would sleep, whether she was going to hear an owl, how—

87

But with a smile he got up and went to the seat in front of them. "Hello there, Mimi, Darlene," he said. "Good to have you back. How've you been since last summer, eh?"

"Oh, blah," said Sue Ellen. "I'm going to take a nap." She leaned back, shutting her eyes. Immediately she felt the hot tears welling, so she dragged some tissue from her pocket and blew hard. She thought about her mother, about the apartment now so far away, so lost to her, about Pop coming in tonight and how he and Momma would sit together talking about her—and about Mady, natch—but mostly, she hoped, about her. She pictured them, and then decided she'd better try to think of something else, because the tears kept coming.

"This train's sooty," she said, blowing again. "Soot like needles. And somebody wrote a bad word on this horrible dirty window. I had to wipe it out before."

"I know," Mady said softly. "Want a candy bar, Sue Ellen?"

"Where'd you get a candy bar?"

"Momma gave me one for each of us this morning."

"Oh, boy. Sure."

It was late afternoon before the train arrived at the right station in Vermont.

"Vermont, yet," Sue Ellen grumbled. "Why not

China? Why not the North Pole?" She felt helpless and hopeless this far from home, and doggedly followed directions, climbing into a waiting bus, not even bothering to see if Mady was with her. What difference did it make?

While she'd been asleep—she'd finally dropped off to the swaying and clacking of the train—Mady had made friends with the counselor, Maria, and after Sue Ellen had wakened, it was Maria this and Maria that until Sue Ellen was just about ready to yell the bad word she'd wiped off the window. She was hot, stiff, and achy. She was starved, but sort of sick-feeling too.

And still it was just today. Still it was only Wednesday.

Mady didn't sit next to her on the bus. A short blonde girl with chocolate at the corners of her mouth plopped into the next seat and said, "Aren't you just *dying* to be there? I'm so hungry I could eat a pig. Alive. Didn't you hate and *despise* that train? I've seen cleaner garbage trucks. I'm going to write and tell Daddy I will *not* take that train back. Not a *chance*."

And I, thought Sue Ellen, am going to write and tell Pop I will *not* stay in camp. Not a *chance*. "What are you going to do to get back?" she asked. "Walk?"

"Eeek! Don't even mention walking. They have

us hiking all *over* the place and my feet hurt from it already. No, I'm going to tell Daddy I have to fly back, naturally. Do you fly much?"

"Only a kite."

The blonde found this hilarious, which had the effect of making Sue Ellen feel better than she had for hours.

"What's your name?" the blonde girl asked, still giggling.

"Sue Ellen Forrest. What's yours?"

"Ida Stansyk. Yours is prettier." The blonde sat up. "We're there. I mean, here."

The bus turned in through some tall wooden gates. A sign decorated with a brightly painted orange-and-black bird swung overhead:

CAMP ORIOLE

Sue Ellen, heart and stomach plunging, closed her eyes as the bus, with a growl of shifting gears, started up the hill.

I won't look, she thought, as the roar of campers' voices rose around her. I just won't. She wished that she could just keep her eyes closed for the whole two weeks and only open them when the bus was facing in the other direction, taking her back along the road toward the station, toward the train, toward home.

Chapter Eight

When Sue Ellen had fallen asleep on the train, Mady sat with her head back, looking drowsily into the future. Since she'd never read a book about a girls' camp or seen anything about one on television, there was nothing for her to refer to, but vaguely she pictured tents with flags flying above them, and mild wild animals wandering freely.

After a time, when Sue Ellen didn't wake up, Mady twisted in her seat and stared back down the aisle. Some kids were singing. That Miss Bur— Maria—had a guitar that she was playing. Her head

91

was thrown back and she was smiling, looking happy and beautiful. Finishing one song, she laid her long fingers on the strings of the guitar and sent her glance around.

Checking everybody, Mady decided. Seeing that we're all all right. Maria's eye caught hers, and the long fingers beckoned.

"Come on," Maria called. "Come and sing with us."

Mady glanced at Sue Ellen, who was either still asleep or pretending to be, then got up and went slowly toward the back of the car.

"Here," said Maria, patting a narrow place beside her. "Squeeze in here. You're—oh, dear. You'll have to tell me again."

"Mady Guthrie."

"Mady. Well, this is Bunny and Gwen and Sally and Alice. And we're all singing. What next, girls?"

"Tit-willow."

"Three Jolly Fishermen."

"Finiculi, Finicula."

"Yes, yes!" they shouted. "Finicula!"

Maria tapped the strings loudly and began to play a melody and to sing with the girls. At first Mady was silent, then she hummed, then when they sang it over again, she put in some of the words.

Listen! Listen! Echoes sound afar!
Listen! Listen! Echoes sound afar!

Finiculi, finicula, finiculi, finicula!
Echoes sound afar . . . finiculi, finicula!

Wondering what in the world it could mean—
finiculi, finicula—Mady sang blissfully. She didn't
see how Sue Ellen could still be asleep in all this
glorious racket. Oh, well, she decided. There's nothing I can do about it. If she wants, she can come here
and sing too.

When they arrived at the station in Vermont,
Mady went with Maria. Sally and Gwen stuck close
by, and when they all got on the bus, the four of
them settled in front. Mady didn't even notice when
Sue Ellen went past, looking for a seat.

"Maria," she said, loving to use the name, "Maria,
are there lots of animals at the camp? I mean, are
there foxes and deer and skunks and frogs and owls
and—"

Maria laughed. "There are, Mady. Of course, you
won't see much of them, except for Ellycat."

"Why not? Why won't I see them? Who's Ellycat?"

"Well—first—because they're wild animals, you
know. They're shy of human beings and stay pretty
much out of the way, and those you named are
nearly all nocturnal. You know what that means?"

"Sure. It means they sleep in the day and go out at
night."

Maria looked impressed, and Mady, pleased, went

on, "I read about animals a lot. I'm crazy about them. Who's Ellycat?"

"A raccoon. She has only three legs, but it doesn't seem to bother her now. Her disposition is so sweet it's sticky. You'll love Ellycat."

Mady knew she would. She already did. "But why does she only have three legs?"

"She was caught in a trap and gnawed her way free."

Mady shivered. "Gnawed her *leg* off?" she said, not wanting to believe it.

"At the first joint. The animal world is pretty harsh and cruel at times, Mady. It's something you have to face if you love them and want to deal with them. I was the one who found her in the woods a little way from the trap, last summer. She was worn out from pain and loss of blood, but even so it was a job, getting her to let me fix her up. She was vicious then. But not any more."

"How did you do it?"

"Gave her a hypo to put her out. She was too weak to resist much. Then we bound up the stump of her leg and gave her some antibiotics and put her in a big cage. It was a long time before she trusted us," Maria went on, "but by the end of the summer the wound was all healed and she was eating from our hands. Even after we left the door of the cage open, she'd go back in there to sleep. She likes to sleep in the daytime, unless someone pays her a visit."

"Can I?"

"You certainly may."

"Where does she stay in the winter?"

"The camp director, Mr. Schering, lives with his family in the old farmhouse that was here before the camp was. Ellycat stays with them. Yes, Alice?"

Mady, left to herself, realized that she had been so busy paying attention to Maria that she'd forgotten to look at the country. And she was, really and truly, in the country now.

Eyes wide, she tried to see in all directions at once. The road they traveled was narrow and curving, and the woods came up to the very edge of it. The woods were practically all Christmas trees of different kinds. Every now and then the trees gave way to open stretches of field, and all of a sudden, as they rounded a corner, Mady gasped to see a herd of cows.

· Real, live cows. They looked huge and peaceful in the sunny grass, chewing and chewing. Their mouths went sideways instead of up and down. She'd tell Momma about that when she wrote to her.

There were flowers at the road's edge and in the meadows. The air that rushed through the open bus windows smelled of flowers.

Then, it seemed almost no time, they turned in through some gates, drove under a sign saying CAMP ORIOLE, climbed a hill, and came to a stop beside a great brown wooden building with a porch running all around it. There was a sign above the big front door: LODGE.

Mady, scrambling out of the bus with the other children, walked a little way from them and stood looking around, taking deep breaths of the country. No tents. But up and down the hillsides, not close together, were a lot of cabins, brown wood like the Lodge. Some distance away, down a sloping meadow, was the lake. It glittered like glass beads. A long wooden platform ran out into the water, and there were boats pulled up on the shore or tied up close to it. Out on the lake was a sailboat skimming along. It had, and she could scarcely believe it, blue-striped sails.

All around the camp grounds girls and counselors went busily from one place to another, carrying tennis rackets, volleyballs, swimming suits, yelling to one another. They ignored the newcomers, except for some who rushed forward with greetings. Those are girls who've been here before, Mady said to herself with envy.

"Are you by any chance still talking to me?" Sue Ellen came up beside her. "By any chance do you remember me, even?"

"Oh, Sue Ellen . . . isn't it heaven? Isn't it beautiful?"

"It gives me the creeps."

"Me too," Mady said dreamily.

"You aren't listening to anything! You're just standing there, being soppy. Oh, I wish I'd *never*—how am I going to get *out* of this?"

"Look at the blue sailboat."

Sue Ellen glanced toward the lake. "The sailboat isn't blue, the sail is. I don't like the country. I don't want to be in the country—" Sue Ellen lifted her chin with decision. "I'm going back."

"Back where?"

"Back home! Back where do you think, you dope, you fool!" Sue Ellen was quivering at Mady's mindless indifference to the fix they were in. "We do have a home, you know. Or have you already forgotten that too?"

"Of course I haven't forgotten," Mady said stiffly. "Does that mean I can't like it here? Oh, Sue Ellen, please, please try to like it. Only two weeks worth. *Don't* talk about going home, please, darling Sue Ellen. I want so much to stay."

"But you *said*—you told me on the train—"

"But that was then, and this is now. Look at it all, Sue Ellen. Look at the trees and the lake and real flowers growing and—"

"I've looked. I hate it. I bet there are snakes here. Anyway, if you don't want to go back, I'll go without you."

"Oh, but you know I couldn't stand it here without you."

97

"You've stood it okay up till now, being without me."

"Only for a little while. You were asleep."

"Not on the bus, I wasn't."

"But—" Mady grabbed Sue Ellen's arm. "Look, look over there, right by that rock. That's a *chipmunk*, Sue Ellen."

"Big deal."

"Look at him sitting up so cute with his little paws against his chest—"

"Will you let go my arm? You're practically breaking it!"

But he was cute, Sue Ellen admitted to herself. A tiny little thing, like a brown mouse with black stripes and this snowy stomach, as if he'd lain down in a puddle of white paint. And he sat there so still, with his head high. She didn't think she'd even have seen him, he was so quiet. Leave it to Mady, though. She'd be seeing animals everywhere. Probably even animals that weren't there. Mady had only found out last year that there weren't any real dragons. A teacher had told her. Sue Ellen didn't think Mady really believed it yet.

There was a sudden, stunning clangor behind them. Sue Ellen started convulsively. "What's that?" she moaned. "What *is* it?"

Mady looked around. "It's that big bell over there. They're ringing it. Bob is."

"What for? Is the place on fire?"

Maria lifted an arm, waving it in a scooping gesture. "Everyone here," she called. "All new arrivals here, please."

"I'm not new," said Ida Stansyk.

"Or me," said Gwen.

"You girls know what I mean," Maria said easily. "All those who just got here on the bus. We'll have time to get you to your cabins before the dinner bell. After dinner, girls, there'll be a swim and then a meeting at the Lodge here, so you can all meet and mingle."

"Swim," said Sue Ellen. "Can they *make* us swim? What happens when we drown?"

"You're going to be as mean as you can, aren't you?" Mady said. "You're going to try to spoil it all."

She and Sue Ellen faced each other tensely for a moment, and then Sue Ellen seemed almost to slump within herself. "No," she said. "No, I won't. I mean, I'll try not to."

Mady took her hand briefly. "We'll have fun. You wait and see."

They joined the others, and then with Ida and Alice followed a new counselor, Hedy, down a winding path to the cabin they were to occupy for the next two weeks.

Mady looked longingly over her shoulder at Maria, who was going uphill with a group of older girls.

99

"You got a crush on her already?" Sue Ellen asked.

"She knows all about animals and she's going to be a veterinarian," Mady said calmly. "She teaches the nature class."

"So that's what you're going to take, natch."

"I would have, anyway."

"Here we are," said Hedy.

The cabin was called Osage. Another wooden sign over the door informed them so. Inside were four double-decker bunks and a cot in one corner with a screen in front of it for Hedy. Two of the double-deckers were already in use, but there was no one in the cabin. Everything looked neat. Since there was just about nothing in here but the beds and a table with an oil lamp on it, it looked, to Sue Ellen, cold and unfriendly. There were mosquito nettings over all the bunks. She took some comfort in that. Underneath that netting, you'd feel cozy, maybe. Sort of protected.

They chose for bunks, and Mady ended up over Alice, while Ida was to sleep above Sue Ellen.

"Too bad you lost the toss," said Ida.

"What'd I lose?" Sue Ellen asked.

"Well, but the chance to sleep on *top*, of course. That way you can look out the window at night and see the moon and the trees and once I saw an owl right on a branch practically at the window."

"You did?" Mady breathed, grateful beyond words that she'd won her toss for the top bunk.

"Suits me fine to be down with a wall beside me," said Sue Ellen. "I don't want to wake up face to face with an owl."

"Girls," said Hedy, "we have just time to get our beds made before the dinner bell rings."

When it rang, sounding somehow louder even than when she'd heard it up there on the hill, Sue Ellen, who was leaning over trying to tuck the blanket in, straightened and hit her head on the top bunk.

"Ah, *gee*," she said. "Oh, darn it, oh, *heck* . . ." She really did want to cry.

"Come now," Hedy said pleasantly. "You didn't hurt yourself, now did you, Sue?"

Sue Ellen, Sue Ellen, my name is Sue *Ellen!*

"No, Miss—uh—no, I —"

"Call me Hedy, Sue. That's easy to remember, isn't it?"

Sue Ellen looked at her stolidly. "Yes," she said. "And I didn't hurt myself. I just got—angry, that's all." The bell rang again, and again she started violently. "I'll never get used to that thing. Not *ever.*"

"Of course you will. It can't be worse than all the city noises you're used to."

"City noises I like."

"Hedy, let's *go*," said Ida, her hand on the cabin door. "I'm starving. Like I'm *dying* of hunger and thirst in the desert. That's the second *bell*."

It developed that each cabin sat at a table in the huge dining room of the Lodge. It further developed that the campers waited on table, and not only that, they set and cleared.

"All the chores of home," Sue Ellen mumbled to herself. "And none of the joys."

"We say grace together, Sue," Hedy informed her.

Sue Ellen glanced up suspiciously, but Hedy was looking perfectly pleasant. Apparently, with her head down, muttering that way, she had looked as if she had been saying grace. Sue Ellen grinned to herself.

The other four girls from the cabin were Diane, Bunny, Miriam, and Darlene. Sue Ellen didn't attempt to sort them out, as she didn't intend to speak to them unless she had to, and then she could always call them "you."

The food was pretty good, and you could have all you wanted. After dinner they helped clear up the dining hall, and then went to the Osage cabin where they got into their bathing suits. They followed Hedy down to the lake front.

There were so many girls and grown-ups of so many ages that Sue Ellen and Mady, sitting close together on a wooden bench, began to be frightened.

103

All day Mady had been entranced and confident, Sue Ellen mainly resentful. Now terror touched them.

"Sue Ellen," Mady whispered. "What—what'll we do?"

"How should I know? You got us into this."

"Can you get us out, please?"

"We could go up to that cabin now and get our clothes on and start for the station."

"Oh, no. It's coming on for night."

"Then tomorrow I'll write to Pop. I'll tell him—"

"Hello, you two. Not even going to put a toe in?"

Maria, brown and long-legged, sat down beside them. "Sue Ellen Forrest and Mady Guthrie . . . two girls planning a getaway."

"How—how did you know?" Mady said, even as Sue Ellen poked her in the ribs for silence. "Stop it, Sue Ellen. I want to know."

Traitor, traitor, double-crosser, Sue Ellen chanted inwardly. One word from this Maria Burburzoom-deyah and Mady falls all over herself forgetting everything else. Grimly, eyes narrowed, Sue Ellen stared in front of her at all the splashing and diving and boating taking place.

"I can tell," Maria was saying. "It's a look, an expression. Unmistakable. It says, 'I want *out.*' "

"You mean a lot of people want out," said Sue Ellen, in spite of her determination to remain silent. It was too good a chance to miss.

"Oh, at first, some do. When you've never been away from home before or out of a big city, it's natural to be overwhelmed by the country just at first, wouldn't you say?"

Sue Ellen refused to say, but Mady insisted she knew just what Maria meant.

"Now, why don't you both come with me and have a bit of a swim? Honestly, it's refreshing, especially after the day we've all put in."

"We can't swim," said Mady, hanging her head.

"Wouldn't you like to learn? Wouldn't you both like to know how to swim by the time you leave here?"

"There won't be time before—" Sue Ellen began at the same time that Mady was saying, "Do you think we could, Maria, in two weeks?"

"Of course you can," said Maria gaily. "Bob Franks is our waterfront director, and he was a champion swimmer at his college. Besides that, he's one of the best teachers you ever met. Come on, girls, let's start by telling Bob you want to learn."

Mady jumped up and trotted at Maria's side without a backward glance. But Maria turned, held out her hand and said, "Coming, Sue Ellen?"

I'm going to write to Pop tomorrow, Sue Ellen promised herself. I'm going to tell him I can't stay here, I want to go home. Meanwhile—well, meanwhile she wasn't going to be called a bad sport by any of these people.

She ignored the outstretched hand but followed Mady's dancing figure down to the water. Mady, who couldn't be trusted at all.

Sue Ellen was aware now that she would have to face her loneliness by herself. But it wouldn't be for long. Just till she wrote to Pop and he came and got her.

Chapter Nine

Bob Franks was standing on the wooden dock, seeing everywhere at once, now and again blowing the whistle that hung on a lanyard around his neck. When the whistle blew, all the kids in the water raised their arms, and Mady noticed everybody was in twos.

"The buddy system," Maria explained. "Every girl has a buddy she stays with in the water. It's a safety measure and makes for quick checking."

Bob turned and smiled at them warmly.

"Good to see you," he said. Sweeping the water with a glance, he said to Maria, "Elaine's on the float, keeping an eye on the boaters, and Louise is with the intermediates. You want to take over here for a bit, Maria? I'll give Sue Ellen and Mady their test right now, and tomorrow they can—"

"We can't pass a test," Sue Ellen interrupted. "We can't swim." She said it almost proudly, because Mady had sounded so ashamed of them.

"You'd like to learn, wouldn't you?"

"No," said Sue Ellen.

"Yes," said Mady, very softly.

Bob didn't argue with Sue Ellen. He smiled and jumped off the wooden pier into water so shallow it barely covered his ankles. "It slopes off very gently," he explained. "How about just standing in here with me?"

Mady went in promptly, Sue Ellen following after a moment. The cool water around their legs was delicious after the hot day, the dirt of the train, the sort of sweaty excitement of everything.

Bob took each of them by the hand and walked slowly into the lake. It did, indeed, get deeper so gradually you were hardly aware of it, and presently they were up to their waists.

"The first thing all swimmers learn is to put their faces in the water and look at the bottom. Want to try?" he invited.

Sue Ellen, skimming her hands over the surface, looked at him carefully. "That's all?"

"That's all, just at first."

Sue Ellen leaned over gingerly, put her nose against the surface of the water, stood up again, and waited for instructions. Mady, to show off, plunged her head down and came up sputtering, sneezing, shaking water from her hair.

Bob laughed. "Too eager, Mady. This is a thing to be done with deliberation. Now, watch." He bent over, lowering his face into the water, and straightened immediately. "That's at first. After you've done that a few times, you'll do it with your eyes open. *Look* at the bottom of the lake. See what you can make out down there. Then you'll breathe out while you're looking at the bottom. Take a deep breath before you lean over, and then breathe *out*. I'm afraid you took a little breath just then, Mady—"

Patiently, easily, giving his whole attention to them and two other nonswimming campers who'd been standing reluctantly on the bank, Bob taught them the satisfaction of being able actually to get your whole face in the water, to keep your eyes open and gaze at the sandy bottom, to breathe out, then straighten up and breathe in, and do it all over again.

The swim was over too quickly, and by the end of it, incredibly to Mady, Sue Ellen had actually learned to float. Mady and the other two girls were still bobbing and breathing when Sue Ellen was

109

stretched out on the surface of the water, arms above her head, floating face downward.

"Golly," said Mady as they made their way back to Osage. "Sue Ellen, I can't get *over* it. I mean, how did you *do* that so fast?"

"It's all in knowing how," Sue Ellen said smugly.

It occurred to Mady that this might be a way of keeping Sue Ellen at camp. If she was proud enough of learning to float, and if the promise of actually being able to swim was sort of dangled in front of her—

"Honestly, Sue Ellen," she said, "you are absolutely marvelously amazing. I mean, *nobody* else learned even half as much as you did. I bet you anything that by the end of two weeks you'll be swimming like a fish, that's what I bet."

"You can just stop that, Mady Guthrie. Because you aren't fooling me one bit. I'm writing to Pop in the morning."

"But, Sue Ellen—"

"But me no buts."

"Well, but I will but you a but!" Mady said angrily. "And anyway, you can't write to Uncle Dan for me."

"So I won't write for you."

Mady, overcome with too much emotion, with too long and strange a day behind her, burst into tears. Alice and Ida and Bunny and Darlene, coming into the cabin, looked at her curiously but said nothing. After them came Diane and Miriam, with Hedy, who drew Mady down on her cot and said, "Now, now. What's your problem?"

There was something about Hedy that dried up tears and struck dumb the tongue. Mady stayed beside her, as it would have been rude to leave immediately, but she didn't answer. She struggled for control and after a moment achieved it. Wiping her eyes with the back of her hands, she mumbled, "I'm tired, that's all."

Hedy accepted the explanation. She got up, clapped her hands, and said, "Dress quickly, girls. Hang your suits on the line outside. We'll all go up to the Lodge for a camp meeting, and then back here. When we get back, climb into pajamas and bathrobes chop-chop, and we'll go up to the wash house together. No dawdling, please. Lights out at eight o'clock."

"What lights?" asked Sue Ellen, looking at the oil lamp.

She didn't intend to be rude. She was asking a question she really wanted answered, but Hedy gave her a quick look that said, "So we're going to have trouble with you, are we?" Mady had seen that look on grown-ups before, when they were looking at kids. She glanced at Sue Ellen and realized un-happily that none of Hedy's expression had been

111

missed. Sue Ellen did *not* like adults to look at her that way, and Mady decided the letter to Uncle Dan was as good as written.

As Osage went up the hill toward the Lodge, girls from other cabins, from Chippewa and Thunderbird and Sioux, came streaming from all directions. It seemed to Mady that everyone in the whole camp was talking to somebody, except Sue Ellen and herself.

Mr. Schering, the camp director, stood at the front of the big meeting room of the Lodge. A fire crackled in a huge hearth behind him. Mady looked at the flames with sleepy fascination. How beautiful it was, the fire. Roaring red and yellow, fringed bluey-green, it flew upward, shooting sparks, sending strange restless lights over the faces of campers in the front row.

Osage, being among the youngest campers, got to sit almost in front. There was singing and then a talk from Mr. Schering about how happy they all were, and how much happier they would be as time went on, and what they were going to do during their stay. Overnight hikes, sports, dramatics . . .

Mady tried to listen but couldn't. She fell asleep, leaning against Sue Ellen, and Hedy didn't notice until the meeting was over and Mady had to be jerked awake.

She fairly stumbled through the short time left until lights out, but as soon as Hedy had extinguished the soft flame of the oil lamp and retired behind her screen to read, Mady found herself wide awake again.

Blissfully snug and private under the mosquito netting, she lay looking around. At first it was still sort of light outdoors, or not really dark. When the darkness came, Hedy lit a flashlight and its faint glow touched the room and the rafters mysteriously.

Mady stared out of her window. She knew immediately when they appeared what the fireflies were, having read about them many times. But truly to be looking at them, flicking off and on all over the night, to be hearing the soft dark wind moving in the branches of all those trees out there, and to see, at length, a great orange moon lift itself into the sky—all this gave Mady a kind of happiness that she hadn't known about before.

Suddenly, through the night, came the call of a bugle. Clear, pure, unwavering, the notes of taps sounded over the camp, over the still cabins, the fields, the empty lake, the woods.

Over the world, Mady thought, filled with a beautiful sadness. It was like an angel blowing a horn over the whole entire world.

She found out later that it was Bob Franks who climbed the hill in back of the Lodge every night and lifted the bright bugle to his lips and told them all good night, sleep well.

Sue Ellen, lying rigidly unsleeping beneath Ida's

bunk, heard the bugle and shivered. It was that thing they blew for dead people, for dead presidents and soldiers. Even after it had stopped, she could hear it, echoing in the night. She thought she had never felt so horribly sad and so by herself in her whole life before.

Chapter Ten

In the morning Bob Franks did not blow the bugle to summon the camp from sleep. Mr. Schering rang the big bell. It had a more rousing effect. Mr. Schering had never gotten over his gratification at finding it his duty to make a lot of noise early in the morning. Duly at seven A.M. he picked up a hammer, drove it against the bell, and found the effect most invigorating.

Sometimes he arrived before seven o'clock. No one ever pointed this out to him. Mr Schering did not mind being told that a rowboat needed repair or even replacement, or that fifteen extra pounds of beef would be required for the visiting softball team from Camp Wincapaw across the lake. But being informed that he often rang the seven o'clock bell at six forty-five would have troubled him. In general the counselors of Camp Oriole preferred not to trouble their director.

On the day after Mady and Sue Ellen's arrival, he made it to the Lodge at six-fifty, consulted his watch, shrugged, and banged away.

In Osage stirrings and grumblings took place immediately. Hedy, with a wry glance at her clock, yawned, pushed a hand through her hair, swung her feet to the floor, groped for her slippers, and checked to see that all her campers were responding to the summons.

All were, except for Sue Ellen who slept on. Hedy walked to the side of the cot, patted Sue Ellen's shoulder, and said, "Rise and shine, Sue."

Sue Ellen wriggled, turned on her side, dragged the pillow over her head, and slept.

Oh, well, thought Hedy. Give her the extra ten minutes. But ten minutes later Sue Ellen was still motionless under the protective pillow.

"Sue," said Hedy sharply. "Time to get up."

No reaction.

Hedy shook the flat, slender form, inert on its stomach. "I *said*—hit the deck!"

Sue Ellen pulled the pillow off, rolled to her back,

116

screwed up her face, and looked through slitted eyes at the counselor looming above her. "Isn't this Thursday?"

"Of course."

"Well, I don't get up early Thursdays." She rolled over, taking the pillow with her.

Hedy pulled it off. "What's so special about Thursday? Do you get up early on Friday or Monday?"

"Nope."

"Why, please?"

"Because school's out. I sleep late when school's out."

"You aren't at school now."

"You're telling me."

"Here at Camp Oriole we get up at seven. Sharp. There's much to do."

"Can't it wait?"

"It cannot. You see that all the rest of the girls have already left for the wash house."

"It's dark. Are you sure it isn't midnight? Somebody made a mistake, that's what."

"It's dark because it's raining."

Sue Ellen sat up indignantly. Sure enough, there was a steady pattering on the roof and a rush of water from the eaves.

"It *rains* here?"

"We are not exempt from prevailing weather conditions."

117

"Holy cow. You go to camp, and it rains. I could've stayed *home* in the rain. What do we *do* here when it rains?"

"We have special activities planned for such days."

"I think sleeping late would be a special activi—" Sue Ellen began, but Hedy looked stubborn and stern.

"Out!" she said.

Sue Ellen sighed, opened her eyes as far as they'd go to give her that wide-awake feeling, and struggled to her feet.

"Where to, Lieutenant?"

"The wash house. Wear your rubbers and raincoat. Bring washcloth, towel, and toothbrush."

"Yeah. Sure thing. It'll be the first time I ever wore rubbers to brush my teeth."

The wash house was musty and fusty. Rain streamed past windows which could not be closed and there was a centipede in one of the sinks.

Sue Ellen splashed cold water on her face, shivered, brushed her teeth quickly, and returned across a series of wooden planks to the cabin to dress. Her clothes felt clammy.

In the dining room raincoats and rubbers were parked at the entrance where they dripped and formed a puddle big enough for a mouse to swim in. Hedy, at the head of the Osage table, had a cup of coffee with her oatmeal.

"Can I have some?" Sue Ellen asked.

"Coffee? At your age?"

"Black, please, and no sugar."

"We sometimes have a *little* bit of coffee in a cup of warm milk," Mady said with embarrassment. "Just for fun."

Sue Ellen glared at her, then down at the bowl of oatmeal Hedy had put in front of her. The cereal looked cold and had formed a pale tan crust on the surface.

"I can't eat this."

"Oh? What would you like instead?"

"Coffee and doughnuts."

"We have doughnuts on Sunday," said Hedy. "Thursday is oatmeal day." She spoke as if it were Memorial Day or something equally unalterable.

"Well, I won't eat this," said Sue Ellen.

The other girls looked interested, but Hedy only said indifferently, "Then have some toast instead."

Sue Ellen took a piece of cold toast and bit on it disconsolately.

Outside the rain poured down. Sue Ellen, looking through the window, could see millions of leaves hanging slippery and drippy. There was grayness all the way down to the lake. No swimming. The only thing in the place that promised to be fun.

"What do we *do?*" she asked again.

Hedy, not answering directly, said, "Girls, after beds and clean-up, we are all to meet in the Lodge

119

for morning activities. Obviously, there will be no flag-raising this morning. However, by noon it may clear up."

"This isn't going to clear up until Thanksgiving," said Sue Ellen.

Hedy fixed her with a cool, brown stare. "Let me say now, Sue, that there will be days here when it rains. Like everywhere else. And there will be days when things do not go as smoothly and pleasantly as we could wish. But we make the best of things. That's the camping spirit."

"Some have it, and some don't," Sue Ellen muttered.

All around the table, eyes turned toward her.

"Apparently you do not," Hedy continued. "But if there isn't, in all of us, the camp spirit, there is another device to make such days as this tolerable, even pleasant."

Sue Ellen said nothing, but Diane asked, "What's that, Hedy?"

"Manners, Diane," said Hedy, looking at Sue Ellen. "Simple manners."

Sue Ellen felt the blood rise to her cheeks. After the way Momma and Pop had brought her up to be so polite! After the way Mr. Carmondy, the school principal, had said, "Sue Ellen, Mrs. Forrest, is one of our most courteous students. An example to others."

That shows how much you know about anything,

Sue Ellen thought, staring back at Hedy. She looked at Mady, who *knew* how polite she was and that even Mr. Carmondy had said so.

"For goodness' sakes, Sue Ellen," Mady said nervously. "Do you have to be such a crab?"

By the time the beds were made and the floors swept at Osage, Sue Ellen was not speaking to anyone. But she walked up to the Lodge with Mady.

"I wish we had an umbrella," said Mady.

"What good's an umbrella in a place where it rains sideways?"

"*Oh*. Oh, Sue Ellen—you're a—a drip!"

Mady flounced off, leaving Sue Ellen to mount the steps to the Lodge by herself.

Inside, in the big fireplace, a fire was burning. It didn't actually make the huge room warm, but was cheerful as a basket of kittens.

Sue Ellen moved close to it.

"Attenshun!" said Mr. Schering, then smiled to let them know that he was kidding with the Army attitude.

Like heck he's kidding, Sue Ellen thought. The whole place reminded her of TV broadcasts about guys at Fort Dix, learning to salute and keep their buttons shiny.

"You will now each get a balloon," said Mr. Schering. "Over in the corner there." He pointed. "You will also find paints. Blow up your balloons and then paint on them the face of anyone you wish.

121

Then we will place them at the end of the hall and throw darts at them."

There were squeals of enthusiasm and all rushed to paint on faces, or daubs intended for faces, of people they'd like to throw darts at.

"Who're you doing?" Sue Ellen asked Mady, who was painstakingly and rather handsomely drawing a face on her blue balloon.

"A boy."

"What boy?"

"Any boy. They're all horrible."

Mady, after a bit, looked at Sue Ellen's haphazard creation. "Who're you doing?"

"Mr. Kusack."

"Sue Ellen, you are awful!" Mady cried. "You aren't really going to try to be nice at all. You *said*. You told me you would, and you aren't even trying!"

Sue Ellen momentarily felt ashamed. "Okay, Mady. I'm sorry. I'll start over again. It's just this rain."

"It isn't anybody's fault it's raining."

"I know. I said I'm sorry. I'll make my face our landlord."

"That's better," said Mady. Their landlord was the one, she guessed, who let the furnace go out in the winter at home. He deserved to be painted on a balloon and have darts thrown at him.

When the darts had left all balloons in a state of
shriveled dampness, there was ducking for apples.

Great sport for a rainy day, Sue Ellen thought,
but in view of her promise to Mady didn't say so.
But she refused to duck. When that and Pin-the-

Tail-on-the-Donkey and a few other games were over, the campers were told to use the rest of the morning on projects of their own.

Mady found a book and settled down to read. Sue Ellen, after wandering around awhile, got some paper and some of the paint that was left and told Mady she was going to make a picture book.

"You are?" said Mady, interested. "What about?"

"Colored people. That's what the name of the book is going to be. *Colored People*."

Mady was surprised. Usually Sue Ellen steered away even from any talk about colored people, and now she was—

"I'm going to have purple people in it, and green people, and cherry-colored people, and . . . and polka-dot people. *All* sorts of different colored people."

Mady laughed. "That should be great, Sue Ellen. Really."

"I know," Sue Ellen said confidently. "I wish I could draw better. Just the same it's going to be a good book. People *striped* different colors, how about that?"

Mady thought that would be marvelous. "Are you going to have words?"

"No. No words. Just all these people, different colors."

Mady read, and Sue Ellen worked on her book until the lunch bell rang, and just as it did, the sun came out from the clouds—dazzling, warm, making the ground steam and the air smell grassy fresh. Sue Ellen put her book in a brown paper bag she'd found, and when they went to the cabin to get ready for swimming, she hid it under her pillow.

"Aren't you going to show it to anybody?" Mady asked, not seeing how Sue Ellen could resist.

But Sue Ellen shook her head. "It's not for anybody here. It's for Pop and Momma. For your momma too."

As so often happened Mady found herself wishing she had thought of it first, and as usual tried to content herself with being proud of Sue Ellen. She was pretty sure that Sue Ellen was going to be famous some day. She didn't know at what. It was just this *feeling* she had.

After the swimming period Mady and Sue Ellen walked back up the hill together.

"That was *good,* the way you floated," Mady said. "The rest of us are still looking at the bottom. Except I can't even open my eyes yet and look. I guess you're the best swimmer, all right."

"I'm still going to write to Pop."

Mady grabbed her arm and they halted on the path.

"Oh, Sue Ellen, please wait a bit. Wait until Saturday, *please?* If you write on Saturday, then Uncle Dan will get the letter Monday, and then he'll come up for you—for us—and I'll go with you.

Honestly. I won't complain or anything. But, please —just till then?"

"Well . . ." Sue Ellen said slowly, "well . . . just till Saturday. But *only* till then," she warned. But Mady was already running up the hill to join the others.

Then, before she had a chance to write, in the Saturday morning mail came a letter from Mr. Forrest to Sue Ellen. He said he'd decided to take Mrs. Forrest on a little vacation.

"She hasn't had a vacation," his letter said, "in a dog's age, and this seems a good time, with you girls safely tucked away in the forest. We'll be gone for a week, to Atlantic City maybe. Mady's mother will be here in case you should have to get in touch with us. Do not worry, Sue Ellen, we won't leave until after Momma finds her birthday surprise on Monday morning."

Sue Ellen waved the letter at Mady. "Now, do you see? See what you've done! If you'd let me write before, this wouldn't have happened. This way we *have* to stay another week."

"Don't you want your momma to have a vacation?"

"Sure I do. Of course. It's just—oh, well, what the heck. I guess I can sacrifice myself that much."

Mady, reading a lovely long letter from her own mother, said nothing. But joy was going off in her like firecrackers. It was too bad about Sue Ellen, of

126

course. Apart from swimming and that secret picture book she was making, Sue Ellen took no fun in anything. She didn't sing when they had singing around the campfire. She didn't care if her side won the softball game. She didn't *join* with anybody.

Mady was sorry about Sue Ellen and pretty sure she ought to be sorrier. But she was too happy to be sorry, really, about anything.

Chapter Eleven

It was the free rest period. That meant the campers could do anything they wanted that was quiet. They could read or sleep or write letters. They could even leave the cabins altogether if they wished, but not to meet and talk or play games.

Over the whole camp was a wonderful stillness. Mady, wandering slowly uphill toward a place she'd found, thought that maybe this was the best time of all. Except perhaps for bedtime, when often she stayed awake for a long while, looking out of her window at the moonlit night, at the fireflies, waiting to see an owl, or hear one, thinking . . .

But this hour was wonderful too. The flagpole in front of the Lodge, now far below her, stood up white and spirey. Very far away in the village the tiny spire of the church, that she could just now make out thrusting through the trees, seemed to echo the flagpole. The flag itself hung motionless.

There wasn't a sound from any of the cabins. Only a faint clatter from the kitchen at the back of the Lodge. Only the sound of birds calling from the depths of the woods. They sounded sleepy, as if they too were having a rest period and only called out a little, now and then, from habit. The grass was hot and dry and fragrant with an odor Mady knew she would love and remember all her life. The smell of grass and pine trees in the hot summer sun.

I never want to leave, she thought passionately. Not ever, ever.

Grasshoppers sprang before her as she walked. There were so many, shooting in all directions, that it reminded her of sparklers going off on the Fourth of July. Once she sank to her knees and waited patiently until a grasshopper leaped to the back of her hand, as he would have leaped on a weed or a rock. She peered down at him, loving his little popeyed face that seemed, she thought, to be looking up at her. His long back legs angled upward, and she could feel them grip her skin as he prepared for

129

flight. He leaped in a great arc and was lost to her in the high grass.

She wandered on.

She had found this place, and no one else ever came here. You had to crawl under a thicket of bushes and inch around a big rock that stuck out into a brook. When you got to the other side of the rock, there was a place, like a tiny room roofed with branches, that the brook ran through.

Here, quite alone, purely happy, Mady spent her free rest periods. She hadn't even told Maria about it. She wanted to know that when she went away it would still be here, still be secret, still be hers. When she was back in the city, she would be able to think about it as if it were waiting, and only for her.

"You can come, of course," she said aloud to a toad who sat a few feet away on the moss. "You can look after things." He studied her with popping, heavy-lidded eyes, throat pulsing so fast it was past counting. He didn't seem to mind her presence. Even when she moved and lay on her stomach to look in the water, he remained, still as a little brown stone.

The brook fell bubbling like soda water from a ledge of mossy rock, then formed a little pool, then slid over some smooth stones and away down the hill to the lake. The water going over the stones looked glossy, and in the pool slivers of fish scurried around ceaselessly. When Mady put her hand over the pond, they sank to the bottom, and when she drew back they rose again, like a network in the water. She played this game with them, deciding that they liked it.

Presently she turned on her back and lay on the spongy ground pine, looking up through the branches to the sky. For a while she didn't even think she was thinking. She took deep breaths of the sun and leaf and moss and pine scented air, as if she could store it, keep it. As in a way she was going to do. Maria was helping her to make a terrarium, a little bit of this part of the world that she was going to take home with her.

She had moss in it, and pipsissewa and wintergreen and partridge berry and a rattlesnake orchid. Maria said they hadn't finished yet. There was still room in the careful arrangement for a sprig of maidenhair fern.

"One of the most rudimentary of plants, Mady, and one of the prettiest. A survivor of the Coal Age, and just about indestructible. Even if it seems to die, it resurrects itself in a miraculous way."

That was how Maria talked, so that everything became lively and exciting. Of course sometimes she explained things so much that it prevented Mady from understanding, but even then she liked to listen.

Maria said there was also going to be room for a tiny pine tree.

"A tree?" Mady had gasped. "A real tree?"

"A real tree. We'll find one not more than two or three inches high."

And she told Mady how the partridge berry, now all green, would flaunt a brilliant berry in the autumn; and how the bell-like fragrant flower on the pipsissewa would fall and leave a green berry in its place; and that the rattlesnake orchid, now a tiny, fuzzy, finely striped plant, would grow tall and throw out a white flower.

"An orchid?" Mady had breathed.

"A wild orchid."

Sometimes when she was here in this secret place, Mady thought about her father. Not in a way that hurt. She decided peacefully that he would have liked this place as much as she did.

She looked around for the little toad, but he had gone his way. Mady decided she had better go hers too. She was supposed to play softball this afternoon. After the game she'd go to arts and crafts with Sue Ellen. I'll make something for Momma, she decided, going down the hill. A lanyard. Or a little key case stamped with Indian designs. She had to make something to bring back for her mother. All the kids did. Besides, she wanted to bring home something besides the terrarium, because she was quite sure that even if she should give it to her mother, they would both know who the terrarium was really for.

She stopped suddenly, in the middle of the path,

stricken with grief. A dead chipmunk lay tossed to one side by some animal or other that had killed it and gone on.

She got down, sitting on her heels, and studied the minute delicate form that lay with head lolling, paws curled, its tiny flame snuffed out.

"Ah, darling," she said mournfully. "What a pity . . . what a pity."

The animal world is raw and cruel, Maria had said, and Mady, for all her wish to deny it, knew that Maria was right.

But to *see* it, to see what had happened to this little creature who had been so gay and darting and now was . . . was gone. Oh, it was sad, sad. Even as she squatted there another chipmunk dashed across the path, tail up, and plunged into the grass as if on an errand of great importance. There were lots of chipmunks in the world. And yet . . . that didn't seem to help. *This* chipmunk was dead.

Mady got out her handkerchief, tipped the little body onto it with a stick, then stepped off the path and dug a shallow hole. She put the shrouded figure in, covered it up, arranged a cross of sticks flat on top of the grave. She had nothing to fasten the sticks together with, so the cross wouldn't last long. But perhaps having it there just a bit was enough. She tried to think of some nice prayer to say, and after a moment whispered, "God rest you merry, Chipmunk."

133

She got up and continued her walk down to the cabin, feeling gentle and sad.

Ida Stansyk met her outside Osage, with Bunny and Darlene.

"Hey, guess what? We're all going to have to do a play for the big bust-up Saturday night."

"What big bust-up?"

"The Saturday night before each two-week period is up we have this sort of camp fracas. Skits and stuff. Each cabin does its own. What a ball, huh?"

Mady brightened. "Yeah. That'd be fun. What sort of play?"

"I thought maybe something from *Winnie-the-Pooh*. You *do* know the Pooh stories?"

"Yes," Mady said coolly. "I know Pooh."

"Oh, good. Then you and Sue can help pick. I mean, we'll all pick, but you two can too," she said generously.

That's big of you, Mady thought. It was the sort of thing Sue Ellen would have said, but Mady would only think.

"You know," Ida was going on enthusiastically, "you could be Christopher Robin, if you wanted. I'd lend you my waterproof hat. And my books."

Mady felt a stirring of excitement. Of course, everyone would have to vote, she supposed. Ida didn't run everything, even if she thought she did. But, to be Christopher *Robin*—

134

"And I have another *neat* idea," Ida continued, giggling. "We have our Eeyore made to order."

"Who?" said Bunny.

"Sour Sue, natch. She's grouchy enough, John knows."

Mady took a deep breath. She did not want to get into arguments with anybody in this camp. All she wanted was to be here, to have fun, to have friends, to be *part* of it all. Wavering between that great, that huge desire and the instant sense of outrage she felt for Sue Ellen, she stood facing Ida, who liked her, who'd said she could be Christopher Robin.

Loyalty won.

"Will you please not call her Sour Sue," Mady said in a clear tone. "She is not grouchy, she's sad. And her name is Sue *Ellen,* do you hear?"

135

Chapter Twelve

So far as Sue Ellen was concerned, from the day Pop had missed hitting Mr. Kusack on Park Avenue, things had gone from bad to worse. Now there was no way out at all. Mady had tricked her into coming here, then tricked her into delaying her letter to Pop, and now she was stuck. Because if Momma and Pop stayed away a week, the way Pop had said, then they wouldn't even be home until the two weeks were just about up.

It was hard to believe that the two weeks would ever, in fact, pass, but Sue Ellen supposed they would, since every other two weeks of her life had always been over in just two weeks.

Well, she decided, lying on her bunk during the free rest period, well—what the heck. Next Tuesday at this time will be the last Tuesday I'll ever see this place. Next Tuesday at this time we'll be leaving tomorrow. I'll get through it somehow. I can think about how Momma and Pop are having fun. And the swimming's good. And my book. She felt under her pillow, touching the brown paper bag. Hedy had asked her once what she was hiding there, but Sue Ellen had looked so threatening that even Hedy was quelled.

There were some things in life that *had* to be just a person's own. For Sue Ellen this book she had thought up all by herself was one. She would share it when the time came with Mady and her mother, with her own dear Pop and Momma. But not with anyone at Camp Oriole. The other day, alone in the arts and crafts shop, she'd done a pageful of checkered people, yellow and black. It made her smile now, thinking about it.

Just the same, between now and that beautiful Wednesday of next week there lay an overnight hike, which she was dreading, and days and days of jolly camping spirit and experience. Days of loneliness too. She didn't have a friend. Mady wasn't her friend, not any more. Mady just about ignored her.

137

From being ablaze with anger to cold with scorn about this, Sue Ellen had passed to a state of wistful longing for the olden times of stringing beads and cruising the ten-cent store and flying the kite off the roof with Pop.

It seemed so far away now—home. It seemed hard to believe that once Mady had listened to everything Sue Ellen said, had followed without question Sue Ellen's decisions.

Ungrateful, that's what she is, Sue Ellen thought, but couldn't summon up a warming rage. Instead, she felt an awful hurt inside her that Mady had slipped so easily away and didn't seem to care or to remember the way they used to be.

Hands under her head, Sue Ellen lay and stared up at the springs of Ida's bunk. Hedy was asleep on her cot behind the screen. Darlene and Bunny were in their bunks, writing letters. Everyone else had gone out to spend the free rest period someplace else.

Sue Ellen wondered where Mady went at this time. She never said, and Sue Ellen wouldn't ask. But the trouble with starting out by not asking things, by refusing even to talk unless it was absolutely necessary, was that the more time went by, the less you could ask or talk. It was like sinking slowly into a hole of silence, the way Alice had descended slowly down the rabbit hole.

If it hadn't been for Bob Franks and the swimming, Sue Ellen didn't know what she would have done, since the book had to remain a secret. It wasn't that the counselors, even Hedy, didn't try to draw her out, didn't try to find out why she was so "prickly," as Bob said.

They did try. And she didn't *know* why she was so prickly and couldn't answer them.

"I guess I'm not a country person," she'd said to Bob. "I grew up in New York City, and that's where I want to be. Besides," she'd added dramatically, "I'm afraid."

"Afraid of what?"

After a long silence, during which she realized that what she meant was not afraid but lonely—which she would never admit to—Sue Ellen had said, "Snakes."

If he had taken her seriously that time, she might have gone on to tell him about—about her *outsider* feeling. And then he could have got her, maybe, to start talking and sharing. To sing, for instance. When they were around the camp fire and everybody else was singing, she couldn't, because she'd started out by refusing to and now didn't know how to start without seeming to give in.

Sue Ellen never gave in. Even when she wanted to, even when she needed to, she did not give in.

But Bob, that day, had laughed as if she'd been making a joke. "Honestly now, Sue Ellen," he'd said. "How many snakes have you seen since you

139

arrived?" When she remained silent, he coaxed pleasantly, "Any at all?"

"At the Nature Center there's a snake," she'd offered defiantly. "Mady told me so. She says it's *monstrous*." Mady had said it was big and beautiful. "She says it's *hideous!*"

"That poor old Roger? Snug in his cage and harmless as only a blacksnake can be harmless?"

"He's huge. And he could escape."

She had known she was getting deeper and deeper into nonsense. *Help me!* she'd entreated him silently, looking up into his face. He seemed so able to help people.

But he'd gotten busy then with a new group coming to swim, and Sue Ellen had gone up to arts and crafts to draw black and yellow checkered people. After that she just talked to him about swimming.

Now the swimming . . . that was great. She'd never known until now what a joy, what a smooth, delicious joy it could be to float, to take at last your courage and strike out in deep water and find that you weren't afraid, weren't going to sink and drown. Bob had said that in two weeks he'd have her really swimming, and she knew it was so. She remembered that day at the city pool when she and Mady had lumbered along, hands on the bottom, pretending to swim. It made her laugh now.

Well, if this place wasn't worth anything else—

140

and it wasn't—at least she'd have gotten this. What she'd do with it back in New York City, she didn't know. Getting to a swimming pool wasn't something that happened every day. In fact, it had happened to her only once. Just the same Bob said that once you learned you never forgot, and that would be something she'd have and could think about and look forward to when she got home. If she ever got back to that swimming pool, she'd slide down that marvelous slide into the deep water.

Home. Sue Ellen turned to face the wall. If she could only go to sleep. . . .

Yesterday had been Momma's birthday. Pop would've given her the note of directions, and she'd have followed them and found the cookbook. In her mind Sue Ellen went over the different recipes, recalled just how the little drawings looked. She was not very good at drawing, but just the same her art teacher at school said she had "style." Her art teacher seemed to think that style was even better than good drawing, and maybe that was so.

How *pleased* Momma must have been!

She hugged another satisfaction to her. Mady had forgotten to send a birthday card to Momma. Of course, Sue Ellen had been careful not to remind her. In all that new-found love for Maria and Ellycat and the woods and the whole darn bag, Mady had forgotten to remember the person who'd been so

141

good to her. Sue Ellen took satisfaction in this. She suspected that was mean of her and didn't care at all. That'd show Momma who really loved her. That'd show them all.

"Hey, *psst!*"

She turned her head slightly and peeked under her arm to see who was at the cabin door. It was Ida, gesturing for Darlene and Bunny to get off their bunks and join her outside. She ignored Sue Ellen and so did Bunny and Darlene as they crept carefully out, not waking Hedy.

Maybe they think I'm asleep too, she thought. But they were pretty dopey because they started talking right outside. Through the chinks in the wall, Sue Ellen could hear all they said. She could even, if she applied her eye to a chink, see them.

"We're going to have to decide about our play," Ida was saying.

"What play?" said Bunny.

"Oh, come on. You remember from last year. The Saturday night before a two-weeks is up, each cabin has to give a skit of some sort. So we have to decide what to give. I'm," she added, "for Pooh—some Pooh story. But we all have to vote. Anyway, I'm staying another two weeks, so I'll get another chance."

"Me too," said Darlene. "I'm staying. So's Alice and maybe Miriam. How about you, Bunny?"

"Nope. I'm going to take a trip with my parents,

142

soon as I get home. We're going to Rockport, Maine, to vis—"

"Well, let me tell you," Ida interrupted, "I can hardly wait for *this* two weeks to be up, so we can have our cabin to ourselves again. I don't mean you, Bunny. And that little Mady is darling. Kind of off the rails about Old Mother Nature, but so *cute*. Only boy-oh-boy, can I ever see the last of Sunshine *Sue* without breaking down!"

They giggled and said hush and giggled some more.

Sue Ellen, her face hot with horror, lay still and had to hear.

"We could do *The Secret Garden*," said Darlene, getting down to business. "That's my favorite book."

"Chippewa did that last year, silly. Anyway, it's too long and complicated for a skit. Don't you remember them? They were *grisly*."

"How about *In Which Tigger Comes to the Forest and Has Breakfast?*" said Bunny. "I think Ida's right. Pooh is the best to do."

"That's a *good* one," Ida agreed. "Hey, here comes Mady. Let's tell her. Hey, guess what? We're all going to have to do a play for the big bust-up Saturday night."

Sue Ellen, rigid, wretched, afraid to stir for fear of letting them know she'd heard, lay in pain, eyes blurred—not with tears but with a sort of dizziness. In a strange way she even got sort of deaf and didn't

143

hear them for a while. Then, just as strangely, Ida's voice came through again, thin and sharp as a paring knife.

"We have our Eeyore made to order," she said, giggling.

"Who?" said Bunny.

"Sour Sue, natch. She's grouchy enough, John knows."

Sue Ellen tensed the length of her slim body, waiting for Mady's reply. It seemed a long time coming. Long enough for Sue Ellen to know that Mady was torn, that she was leaning toward the fun of giggling with this gaggle of girls, being one with them in making fun of the outsider.

Then Mady said, "Will you please not call her Sour Sue. She is not grouchy, she's sad. And her name is Sue *Ellen*, do you hear?"

Weakly, Sue Ellen turned on her stomach, buried her face in her arms, and pretended to be asleep when they came in.

In the afternoon after the softball game Mady went with Sue Ellen to the arts and crafts shop—at the time when Sue Ellen liked it best, when there wasn't anybody else there.

Mady started a lanyard. Sue Ellen helped her to pick her colors of plastic cord—she took pink and green—and then showed her how to get started, how to do a square stitch. Sue Ellen was making a very

144

fancy lanyard for her father, but Mady's was quite simple.

They worked together happily, almost as if they were back home stringing beads.

"For John's sake," said Ida, bursting in breathlessly, "where've you two *been?* Okay, all right, you've been *here*. But I've been looking *every*where. We have to get together and decide about our play. Down in the cabin. Come *on*."

Taking her time, Sue Ellen folded her materials together, stored them in her box. "You can have this box, Mady," she said. "We put them on the shelf here, and then when we come back—"

"Will you come *on!*" Ida demanded. Her eyes were wide and starey and Sue Ellen decided that meeting them was like looking into the headlights of a car. She started to say so, then changed her mind.

"We'll come when we're ready," she said.

"I'm not even sure I want you in our play," Ida snapped.

"You do the deciding, do you?"

They tensed, and Mady gasped. It seemed that in another moment they'd be rolling on the floor together. Then Hedy, who directed arts and crafts, walked in. She either didn't notice, or pretended not to, the battle that shimmered in the air.

"Mady," said Hedy, sounding pleased. "How nice to have you here. I hope Sue has been a help? I was busy or I'd have been here earlier. On the other hand Sue should be a very good instructor. She's been doing beautiful work."

"She helped me lots," Mády said anxiously. "I'm making a lanyard for my momma. I mean, my mother." She was so nervous, so nervous. Quarrels—anybody's quarrels—made her feel sort of sick. And she knew just how nasty Sue Ellen could be when she was riled up. Only what had got her going this time? "She helped me *lots*," she repeated, and Sue Ellen snorted.

But they followed Hedy back to the cabin, where the rest of the Osage girls were already assembled. They had the two Pooh books, *Winnie-the-Pooh* and *The House at Pooh Corner*, on the table, and were arguing over which chapter to do.

"Now we're all together," Hedy said, "let's see if we can come to a decision about *which* story very quickly. Then we can get on with casting and rehearsals. We'll also have to design and paint our set—a very simple one, of course. And some sketchy sort of costumes. If we had time, of course, we'd do something more elaborate, but in some ways it brings out the mettle of actors to do things in this snappy, spontaneous fashion—"

She was lively and interested and Mady realized that without noticing when it had happened, she'd come to like Hedy very much. Not as much as Maria, of course. But Hedy, in her quick, sometimes impatient way, was nice.

147

The story selected was *In Which Christopher Robin Leads an Expotition to the North Pole.* Partly because it was a good story, and mostly because there were eight girls in Osage, and the members of the Expotition came out to eight too. Hedy agreed to play all Rabbit's friends and relations herself.

"I think I should be Eeyore," said Sue Ellen in a sudden clear voice. "I'm grouchy enough, John knows." When this was greeted with surprised silence, she added, "In fact, you can call me Sour Sue. Unless anybody prefers Sunshine Sue, of course."

The silence continued. Ida, Darlene, and Bunny looked at one another guiltily.

"Well, out with it," Hedy said at last. "Something's cooking, and we might as well find out what it is."

"It's—uh—must've been us," Ida said uneasily.

"We were hacking around before," Bunny offered. "Saying dumb things. I mean, you don't always *mean* the—"

"What dumb things? Who was?" said Hedy.

Ida shrugged. "Some of us."

"Me and Darlene and her," said Bunny.

"Darlene and she and I," Hedy corrected automatically. "What dumb things?"

"Oh, skip it," said Sue Ellen. "What's the diff? They were talking about me, and they were prob-

148

ably right. I guess. I am sort of grouchy, probably," she concluded in a mutter.

Mady looked at her proudly.

"Besides," said Ida. "Eeyore is a *luverly* part. I only wish I was taller because then *I* could play him. I'm sort of grouchy myself, sometimes."

It was an apology, and after a moment Sue Ellen smiled.

"*Hee-haw, hee-haw,*" she said, sounding just the way Eeyore, the old gray donkey, must have sounded in his damp and thistly corner of the forest.

"Fine," said Hedy. "We have our Eeyore. Now, who's to be Christopher Robin? Shall we vote?"

By dinnertime they had the cast selected and had already started rehearsing. Mady, watching Sue Ellen, saw that it was the first time her friend had looked happy since that night when they'd flown the kite from the roof back at home.

Chapter Thirteen

Sue Ellen had come up to the nature center with Mady. She had helped to clean out the hamster cage and eyed Roger, the big blacksnake, nervously, refusing to touch him even when Mady insisted that he felt like velvet and was really affectionate. She had agreed that the salamander was, as Mr. Forrest had told them, a pretty little thing. Sue Ellen refused to touch it, either, but looked with interest as Mady held it on the palm of her hand.

"It's like a tiny little dragon," Sue Ellen said. "Do you suppose it could really live in fire?"

"Of course not," Mady said in a superior way. "That's just a myth. And there aren't any dragons. Not really, you know."

I know, Sue Ellen thought. I just wasn't sure you knew. But she didn't say anything. Just watched as Mady put the salamander gently back in its glass home.

"Want to see my terrarium?" Mady offered.

Sue Ellen exclaimed when she saw it. "I didn't know it'd be so pretty, Mady. It's gorgeous." She regarded it with obvious pleasure and envy.

Indeed, the terrarium, now complete, was as wonderful a thing as Mady could remember ever seeing. The bowl was a large, squat jar that had once held dill pickles, with a square of glass over the top to retain moisture. Planted in the moss, besides the pipsissewa, the partridge berry and wintergreen, the maidenhair fern and the rattlesnake orchid, were two tiny white pine trees. It was hard to believe— still, there they were. Two perfectly shaped little bitty trees.

"Will they grow?" Sue Ellen asked, entranced.

"Not very fast. Not in time for Christmas," Mady said, laughing. She was trying to be offhand, but in truth she was almost achingly proud of her terrarium. Because this was something she and Maria had created. Because it was part of this place, these woods and marshes. She had gotten the partridge berry in her secret place, and the moss. Whenever I

151

look at it, she told herself, I will feel as if I'm back here.

She said it but knew it would not be true. Only being here would ever be enough. Remembering, she thought, will probably hurt, and whenever I look at the terrarium, it will not be as if I was here. It's only going to remind me of all I'm missing. What would her secret place be like in the wintertime—with the brook running under a coat of ice, and snow covering the moss, drifting down through the pine branches?

"Golly," said Sue Ellen jealously. "That's much nicer than my lanyards and my key case."

For a moment they both thought that Sue Ellen was going to suggest that she too make a terrarium. I should offer to help, Mady thought, and felt a wave of selfish rebellion. It was always Sue Ellen who made things, who was artistic. This was the very first time that Mady had done something Sue Ellen hadn't thought of first. And she hadn't even really entirely made it herself. No, Sue Ellen just couldn't—

"Your key case is *gorgeous,*" she said. "And Uncle Dan is going to be crazy about his lanyard. It's so *com*plicated."

"Oh, sure," said Sue Ellen. "Sure thing."

"Besides, your book is better than this," Mady said, not believing it.

"No, it isn't," said Sue Ellen, not believing that.

152

They smiled at each other suddenly.

"Let's see if Ellycat is about," Mady suggested, taking a couple of small apples from a dish near the window.

The door of the raccoon's cage was open, but Ellycat had chosen to remain at home. She was curled in a far corner, a plump cushion of rough grizzled fur, the beautiful striped tail wound around in such a fashion that there was no way to tell where her head was.

"Isn't she sort of big?" Sue Ellen asked doubtfully. "I thought a raccoon was one of the smaller animals."

"Her fur makes her look bigger than she really is," Mady explained. "Still—Ellycat isn't *wizened.*"

"Wizened," Sue Ellen repeated. She guessed that was one of Maria's words. Mady had taken to imitating Maria's way of talking, of walking. Sue Ellen imagined that Mady probably even tried to think like Maria. Mady was a city girl, and city girls, even city girls who were crazy about animals, just did not pat blacksnakes and say they were full of affection. But Maria liked snakes, so Mady liked snakes.

"Wizened," she said again.

"It means all shrunk up. Shrunken," Mady explained.

"She doesn't look shrunken," Sue Ellen agreed, studying the fat furry ball that now began to stir in its corner. Sue Ellen backed off slightly.

153

"Ellycat," Mady called softly. "Come on, lovey. Come and I'll give you an apple. Elly-elly-elly-cat . . ."

The great bundle of fur shook itself, grew still, seemed to ripple, rose at length, and became a large animal with a masked face turned inquiringly toward the two girls.

"He looks like a thief," said Sue Ellen.

"She. *I* think she looks like a lady going to a masquerade ball."

Sue Ellen laughed, and the sound seemed to force Ellycat to a decision. She humped forward on her three legs, through the open door toward Mady, who was kneeling on the ground, holding an apple out. Ellycat walked over and put her two front paws on Mady's knees, turned her face up, and studied Mady's in a grave, attentive way.

"Golly," said Sue Ellen. "She wants to say something, doesn't she?"

"She is saying something."

"What?"

"She's saying, 'Where's my tea?' "

"Oh, *Mady!*"

"No, honest. Just about this time every day Maria brings her some tea and Danish. That's why she won't take the apple."

"Oh, for the luva mud. Tea and Danish for a rac-*coon.*" These animal people were the living end.

"Hi, girls."

They turned, and there was Maria with a wooden mug and a Danish pastry on a tray.

"Ready for your snack?" Maria said to Ellycat, and Sue Ellen goggled.

But she was enchanted by Ellycat, by the long dark fingers that closed around the small wooden mug, by the thrust of the pointed snout as the raccoon thirstily drank the tea.

Looking from the raccoon to Mady and Maria, who hovered over Ellycat like a couple of mommas, Sue Ellen said to herself, "Poor Mady, how she'll hate to go home." For the first time she was glad that matters had worked out so that Mady got her full two weeks of the country.

Ellycat, having noisily disposed of her tea, snatched the Danish pastry from the tray, hobbled agilely back into her cage, and broke off a piece of the cake. She put it carefully into her tray of water and began to pat. As she patted, the piece of cake broke into crumbs and dissolved. Ellycat, in increasing confusion, pawed about for what she knew she had put in there and now could not find. Pushing her long fingers into every corner, she stopped at length, gazed reproachfully at Mady, then climbed into the tray and shoved about with her nose in a desperate search.

"Oh, my, oh, dear," Maria gasped. "We shouldn't laugh, really we shouldn't."

With an effort they composed themselves, and

155

Mady reached into the cage, gently urged Ellycat from the pan, and emptied it of what water was left.

"Now she'll eat the rest of the Danish, and then we'll fill the water tray again," she explained to Sue Ellen. "Usually we empty the dish first, but today I forgot."

"Was she trying to wash the pastry?" Sue Ellen asked.

"That's what it looks like," Maria said. "Raccoons always do that with food if there's water available. Ellycat just doesn't seem to catch on that things like meat and apples can be washed and then eaten, but cake is going to disappear every time."

"She's nice," said Sue Ellen. Maria and Mady nodded proudly as Ellycat, having finished her snack, took one of the apples back to her far corner. Maria explained that raccoons, being nocturnal, spent most of the day asleep.

"We consider it a tribute that she wakes up for us, don't we, Mady?"

Sue Ellen looked at the two of them wistfully. She wished, briefly, that she was the imitating sort. Or even that she wanted to be friends with one of the counselors this way. She was getting to like Hedy. She was crazy about Bob, of course. Every girl in camp was crazy about Bob. But the sort of closeness that Mady and Maria had developed—that was beyond her in this place.

"How's swimming, Sue Ellen?" Maria asked, lean-

156

ing back on the grass, her arms behind her.

"I love it. It's—I don't know how to describe it. I mean, yesterday when I pushed with my feet away from the dock and actually *swam,* with a crawl, I mean, and a good flutter kick . . . it was—" She turned out her hands helplessly.

"It's difficult to put a sensation like that into words," Maria agreed.

"Do you like to swim?"

"Well enough. But that wasn't what I meant. I mean that it's difficult to say what the feeling is of doing a thing really well, you know? But it's one of life's great joys, the knowledge that there is something you can excel at, something you are truly good at. Not that you have to turn into the world's backstroke champion or anything like that. Just something that gives you pleasure and confidence."

"Yes," said Sue Ellen, but what she was thinking was that Maria talked an awful lot.

"And," Maria went on with a smile, "it's made you more resigned to being at Camp Oriole, hasn't it? You don't want to run away anymore?"

Sue Ellen shook her head. "No. But I'll still be glad to get home," she added firmly. "I miss my folks."

Mady turned her head away. She was not going to be glad to be home. It made her heart feel like stone, just knowing that next week at this time she'd be there instead of here. Momma, she thought painfully, Momma, what's the matter with me? It wasn't that she didn't want to see her mother and Uncle Dan and Aunt Lillian. Only she did not want to go home. Not ever? she asked herself. At this moment she truthfully answered, *Not ever*.

There *must* be something the matter with me, she thought, and met Maria's glance, that look she had of seeming to know everything. Maria started to say something, changed her mind, and they sat together in silence for a while, listening to the birds, to distant shouts from the softball field, to their private, unseen thoughts.

Later, after lunch, as she and Sue Ellen walked toward the cabin for rest period, which today was not free and meant they all had to nap, or pretend to nap, Mady looked at the six girls and the counselor in front of them.

Hedy and Sue Ellen and I, she thought suddenly, are the only colored people in the cabin. Most of the time she didn't bother herself wondering about color. Still, you couldn't help noticing, once in a while, couldn't help thinking what it would be like to be white like fat Diane or little sassy Ida or beautiful Bunny.

"Would you like to be a white person?" she said to Sue Ellen, who stopped on the path, looking nonplussed.

"A white person?" For a moment she seemed irritated, and Mady guessed she'd refuse to answer, but after a bit she said seriously, "I'm not sure, Mady. I mean, I guess so. Sometimes. In some ways. But only if I could still be me, Sue Ellen Forrest, my*self*. With my own parents. And I don't see how I could be white and still have my own father and mother for parents, do you?"

Mady had to laugh. "No. It doesn't seem as if that would work out."

They were at the cabin now, and of course Sue Ellen didn't turn the question around and ask if Mady would like to be white. Sue Ellen didn't ask that sort of thing.

But would I? Mady wondered, lying on her side on her upper bunk, looking out the window at all their bathing suits limp on the line, at the long stretch of meadow that led down to the lake, deserted now except for a sailboat out in the middle. It had orange sails.

She supposed her answer would have come out about the same as Sue Ellen's. In a way. Sometimes. She knew it would be easier in lots of ways to be white. But she wouldn't want to be somebody else, not for any reason. And she would not give up her own mother. She and her mother didn't get along in a—a jolly way, like the Forrests. And she couldn't share things with her in the same way that she could with Maria. But Momma and I *belong* together, she thought.

She wished all the business of being colored was as

159

silly and cute as it was in the secret book that Sue Ellen was willing to share with her but with no one else in camp. Now she had put in checkered people and floral people and rainbow people. There seemed to be no end to the sort of colored people Sue Ellen could think of for her book.

Mady sighed, feeling her eyelids droop. It had been such a good morning with Maria and Sue Ellen and Ellycat. Such a good morning. Through her lashes she watched the sailboat skim over the bright and sun-dazzled waters and didn't notice when she stopped watching and slept.

Chapter Fourteen

The evening of the overnight hike had come, and the girls from Osage were singing as they marched. Hedy said that since the days of the Pharaohs people had found it easier to walk or work together if they sang.

"It elevates the spirit, gives tone to the step," she told them, and at the head of the line lifted her strong, smooth voice in a song she'd taught them.

> *Men of Harlech, in the hollow,*
> *Do ye hear like rushing billow,*
> *Wave on wave that surging follow*
> *Battle's distant sound?*

161

'Tis the tramp of Saxon foemen,
Saxon spearmen, Saxon bowmen,
Be they knights, or hinds, or yeomen
They shall bite the ground!

It was a little past five o'clock. The sun, though declining, had a long way still to go. Its rays slanted through the pines, hemlocks, maples, oaks, beeches, and birches. Hedy had them identify the various species. The sun seemed, at this hour of falling away, to enrich the forest fragrance, to dapple light and shadow more sharply. Whenever they stopped for breath, the hikers could hear the vespers of the birds grown fuller, as if they, like the sun, wanted a crescendo upon which to leave the day.

"What're hinds and yeomen?" Sue Ellen asked Hedy, when they'd stopped singing for a while and were marching double through the woods. She and Hedy were in the lead, but the company was brisk behind them, even Diane who'd been complaining all day.

"Hinds, in the feudal ages, were peasants or serfs, beholden to the lord of the manor. Slaves, in other words. Yeomen were freeholders."

"Freeholders?"

"Men born free."

"Who were the Saxons?"

"Very early conquerors of England."

"Were they white people?"

"Oh, definitely. Northern, Germanic types."

162

"So white men were slaves too, once upon a time?"

"They were. And not just in Saxon England. There were white slaves in Greece, in Russia—"

"Funny nobody ever mentions it."

"You'll find it mentioned later on in your history books. Although," Hedy added, "mentioned is about all you'll find it."

Still, Sue Ellen was glad to hear about it. Information like that gave you a sort of different picture of things generally.

They walked on—humming sometimes, breaking again into song—toward Eagle Rock, their camping spot. The sun, now a tremendous pumpkin-colored circle that a person could look straight at, lowered itself behind the trees, turning the branches to black cat's cradles. But still the sky above remained light and the birds continued their evensong.

Diane, all at once, cried out from the rear that she'd gone as far as she intended to. "My feet are all blisters, and my side aches," she wailed.

"Oh, for John's sake," said Ida. "Let's send her back."

"I'm not going back by myself!"

"Boy-oh-boy, what a delinquent juvenile," Ida said with disgust.

"Oh, now," said Hedy.

"She's going to spoil everything. My gosh, you're a pest, Diane."

"Well, you're a pest too!" Diane shouted at Ida.

"You're a pest like an insect! You're a mosquito, a bug! I'm going to put on my insect repellent against you!" She fumbled in her pack for her can of insect spray, while the others stood around and laughed.

Hedy sat down beside her. "Diane, dear," she said. "Listen to me. You really are much stronger than you think. You've just gotten into the habit of saying you can't do things, without ever giving yourself the chance to see whether you can. Now, we'll put some salve on your heels—they aren't really blistered, you know—"

"My blisters start way down deep," Diane said obstinately. "Even a doctor can't always see them when they start, but—"

"We'll put salve on to keep blisters from forming," Hedy interrupted smoothly. "And then you and I will take the rear, very slowly. Bunny, you and Ida know the way to Eagle Rock. You start on ahead and collect wood for the camp fire. Diane and I will be along."

"I want Mady to stay too," Diane whimpered, taking advantage of Hedy's gentle, coaxing tone and the attention she was receiving. "She's *kind*. Not like the rest of them."

An expression of irritation flickered briefly in Hedy's eyes and was gone. Mady, watching, wondered what it would be like to be a counselor here and not a camper. In a way at this moment Hedy

165

reminded her of her own mother. Impatient with laziness or whining, but kind.

They started off, Diane hobbling in the middle. Hedy, her head up, kept getting ahead, dropping back. Everything she did was quick and light. Yes, she's a lot like Momma, Mady thought. Maria, on the other hand, was more like Aunt Lillian. They seemed to like everybody and never got impatient. If Aunt Lillian or Maria had been here now with Diane, they'd have given her a hug and said, "Come along, lovey, there's the girl," and lovey would have come along without another whimper.

The other girls had disappeared quickly, but the three stragglers could hear them singing again.

> *Listen! Listen! Echoes sound afar!*
> *Finiculi, finicula, finiculi, finicula!*
> *Echoes sound afar . . . finiculi, finicula!*

Mady would have preferred hearing the birds, who grew silent at this noisy invasion. Still, she thought, it was a pleasant sound coming through the woods, all those girls' voices and the laughter.

When Hedy, Mady, and Diane arrived at the clearing at Eagle Rock, the fire was already going and the supper things unpacked. They had hot dogs, rolls, little tomatoes, potato chips, cookies, and hot chocolate. Then there was a marshmallow roast. Blackened and hot, runny and sweet, the marsh-mallows—except for those that fell off the sticks into

166

the fire—were eaten in the near dark and accompanied by a sitting-down rehearsal of the North Pole Expedition.

Then they spread their bedrolls and lay down at length to sleep. Far away, sounding almost as if it fell from the dark above them, came the call of the bugle back at camp.

Day is done, gone the sun, from the lake, from the hill, from the sky. All is well, safely rest, God is nigh.

Mady, lying between Sue Ellen and Bunny, looked up past black branches to the sky that was freckled with stars, marbled with the Milky Way.

She thought how far, how far and far away they were, all those stars. Glittering millions and millions of miles from Earth. But she could see them, and Momma, going to work tonight, would see them, and everywhere on this side of the world there would be those same stars shining, and people looking up to see them.

"Sue Ellen?" she whispered.

"Mmm?"

"Are you happy?"

Silence. Then Sue Ellen whispered back, "Sure. It's wonderful, Mady."

Mady sighed and smiled.

"Sue Ellen?"

"Mmm?"

"Do you think we'll be able to come back?"

"When?"

"Next year? Do you think Mr. Kusack will ask us again?"

Another silence. "I don't guess so," Sue Ellen said finally. "I mean, once is enough usually for people doing things. Treats like this."

"Is once enough for you? To come here?"

"I'm sorry, Mady. But I guess so. I mean, I like it all right now, but not again. But you could come back, I bet. They like you here. And they have like scholarships. Maria told me. Or—oh, I guess there'd be a way. Your mother could save some money—"

"If she didn't give me anything for my birthday or Christmas," Mady said eagerly, "and your folks didn't either, then we could save the money for camp, couldn't we?"

"Sure, Mady. You'll work it out somehow. If you still want to, next year."

"Oh, I'll want to. I'll always want to come back."

"But gee," said Sue Ellen. "Don't you want to *see* everybody at home? I mean, I can hardly wait to see Momma and Pop and the dolls. We can go to the ten-cent store Thursday, okay? I get so excited when I think about being home that I—"

Unconsciously, their voices had risen to normal, and Hedy called in a low voice, "Better go to sleep, girls. Breakfast at dawn, just about."

They heard her yawn, and reassure Diane, who

was complaining softly and steadily. "Diane, there *aren't* any wolves in this part of the country, or bob-cats, either. Be a good girl and go to sleep, won't you?"

"I *can't*," came the low lament.

"Then pretend," Hedy said and yawned again. "Close your eyes and pretend you're dreaming all this. Good-night, Diane," she said firmly.

There was silence. Except for the embers of the camp fire falling apart with a sound like cracking glass. Except for the gentle night wind in the trees, and, after a while, eerily, the rippling hoot of an owl close by.

Mady fell asleep in the wonder of being here in the night in the forest, listening to an owl.

Chapter Fifteen

Mr. Forrest was waiting in Grand Central Station, at the head of the ramp, as returning campers streamed up to the embrace of waiting parents. Encumbered with luggage, with bows and arrows, with jars of tadpoles and bunches of wilting wild flowers they arrived, some full of noise and joy, others silent, reluctant.

Sue Ellen, when she saw her father, let out a shriek and ran toward him, leaving Mady behind.

"Pop! Hey, *Pop* . . . here I am! You came your very self!"

She was so impressed, so overjoyed to see him that she wanted to run around and yell at the top of her lungs.

"Oh, boy, oh, boy. Oh, Pop . . . I'm so glad to be back!"

"Humph. That's dandy. But you had a good time? You liked it?"

"Oh, sure, Pop. It was a gas."

Now that she was safely back in New York City, Sue Ellen was prepared to say any good thing about Camp Oriole.

"We were crazy about it," she said, happily stroking his sleeve.

Mady, clutching her terrarium, arrived at his side and looked up at him with wide, wan eyes.

"And Mady O'Grady?" he asked. "She liked it too?"

"I—" Mady took a deep breath and nodded.

Bob arrived with their duffel bags and bedrolls. "Great pair you've got there," he said, shaking hands with Mr. Forrest. "Wish we could talk, but—" He waved a hand toward a milling group of campers and was gone.

Mr. Forrest stooped to study Mady's prize. "And what's this?" he said. "Have you brought the forest home with you?"

"It's—a terrarium, it's called." And it's mine, she said silently. It belongs to me.

171

"Oh, that's what it is. I often wondered what those things were called. I must say, it's the finest one I ever saw."

"She made it herself, Pop," said Sue Ellen. "Mady learned all about nature."

"Maria," Mady whispered. "She taught me."

"Maria," he said. "One of the counselors?"

But Mady had gone as far as she could go. Tears spilled from her eyes, coursed down her cheeks. Mr. Forrest took the terrarium so she could get a tissue and wipe them away.

"She doesn't want to come home," Sue Ellen explained in a loud whisper. "She's been like this all the way down on the train. Cries and stops, cries and stops. I don't know, Pop. Maybe the whole thing wasn't such a good—"

"Come along," said Mr. Forrest loudly. He gave the terrarium back to Mady, and took up their belongings. "If you two will follow me. Your mother is working, Mady. But she'll be home this afternoon as soon as she can. And Momma," he said to Sue Ellen, "is sitting on the stoop holding her breath till she sees you."

"Why didn't she come too?"

"You know your momma. She decided she'd rather be on home ground so she could burst into tears with only the neighbors to see."

"Why'd she cry 'cause I got *back?*" Sue Ellen demanded.

"Emotion," said Mr. Forrest, "isn't something you ask *why* about."

"Did you bring the hack, Pop?"

"You think the Yellow Cab Company has nothing else to do with its fleet than provide transportation for country mice coming back to town?"

"I just thought. Anyway, I'm *not* a country mouse."

"There's a vehicle called a subway over here that makes better time than a taxi anyway. Come along."

On the subway Sue Ellen shouted information in an uninterrupted flow. Mr. Forrest was too interested to interrupt. Mady was so engulfed with loneliness for all she had left behind that she scarcely heard.

She'd stopped crying, but her whole self felt bruised, as if part of her had been cut off and she was supposed to go on without it. They were still there —Maria, Hedy, Ida. Bob would be going back tomorrow. What were they all doing back there, now, right this minute?

But she didn't want to think what they'd be doing. She didn't want to think or feel. She did not know how the days would pass and the weeks and the months, until she could go back and *be* there again. The paths, the fields, the lake, the nature center— they were all in her mind like a picture painted there. And her secret place.

Could a place miss a person? A person who had

173

loved it very much, more than any other place in the world? Could a place feel that a person wasn't there anymore? Would a little brown toad know?

"We had this play that we gave, Pop," said Sue Ellen. "I was Eeyore, and I was great. Mady was Christopher Robin. She was good too. We had flag-raising there every morning, and Sunday mornings we had chapel, and we had to get up even on Sunday early. I designed the set for that play, did I say? Well, I practically did. Hedy did most, I suppose. We had an overnight last Friday. That's a hike. With a cookout and all this singing and marshmallows over the fire. Pop, did you ever see the moon in the country?"

"Well, I—"

"Honest, it looked like a canned peach hanging in the trees. And sleeping on the ground is *the* end, let me tell you. But I'll tell you, Pop . . . I learned to make Bisquick biscuits in a frying pan. I'm going to make some for you tomorrow morning for breakfast."

"Well, that'll be—"

"Maybe not tomorrow. Maybe the next day. Tomorrow I'm going to sleep late. How's Momma? Did you have a good trip? Did you like Atlantic City, what's it like down there? Pop, did Momma *really* like my cookbook I made her? She wrote that she liked it, but did she really?"

"I think she—"

"I made another book in camp. Not a cookbook. This is a picture book, without any words in it. It's called—"

"I believe," said Mr. Forrest, getting up, "that we're arriving at our station."

The streets seemed to Mady more crowded than they'd been before she left. The stores looked bigger and tackier. The air smelled tarry and gritty and sort of sour. The sound of traffic and voices and loud-speakers at store entrances filled her ears to bursting.

These were her streets. She knew them. All her life she'd known them. And now they were like a place she'd never been before. There was the ten-cent store. Sue Ellen gave Mady a happy nudge.

"Looks the same as ever, huh? Let's come over tomorrow."

"I hate it!" said Mady. "I'll never come again."

"Well, I'll be! Well—you traitor, you!"

"Sue Ellen," said Mr. Forrest.

"No, but Pop!"

"Did you get my card from Atlantic City? The one with the seashell stuck to it?"

"Sure. Sure thing. I've got it saved." She glared at Mady. "I *told* you it was a dopey idea, Pop, and you see? Somebody goes off to the cruddy country for two weeks and acts like her whole life was different."

"Perhaps it is," he said, sounding sad. "Places take people that way. You go to a new environment, a strange corner of the world, and it's as if you'd known it all your life. It's as if you recognize something of yourself there, even if you've never seen it before."

Mady looked up at him, tucked her terrarium snugly under one arm, and slipped the other hand in his.

At home, sure enough, Mrs. Forrest was sitting on the stoop with Mrs. Gerez. She did not burst into tears, but laughed and opened her arms wide.

Sue Ellen ran against her with a sob. "Momma! Momma! I'm home!"

"You're home, my lovey. Oh, my, oh, my, how we missed you." Mrs. Forrest rocked Sue Ellen back and forth, then held her off. "You look like a picture. All that sea air did you good, huh?"

"Momma!" Sue Ellen laughed. "We weren't anywhere near the sea. Just a lake."

"You're right, you're right. It's Atlantic City's by the sea. I get mixed up whose vacation I was on. Mady, come here to Aunt Lillian. How's my precious?"

Held in those plump, constricting arms, Mady felt the pain begin to lessen. Aunt Lillian, she said to herself. This is Aunt Lillian.

But upstairs, when Mrs. Forrest said, "Come in with us, Mady. Have a bite till your momma gets home. You don't want to stay in there alone," Mady shook her head.

"I guess maybe I'll unpack or something," she said, knowing she wouldn't.

"Or cry some more," Sue Ellen said impatiently, then shrugged at her mother's frown. "So? It's all she's done all day, just about. She doesn't like us anymore, and she doesn't want to be with us, just because of that old camp."

Mady looked up at Aunt Lillian with appeal. She shook her head without speaking and hoped Aunt Lillian would know that it wasn't so, what Sue Ellen said wasn't so.

"You should be ashamed, Sue Ellen," said Mrs. Forrest. "Mady's a little homesick for the camp, the way you were homesick for home. You wrote it in your letters. I bet Mady didn't talk mean to you when you were homesick."

"Then she isn't homesick, she's campsick. Besides, I've lived at home all my life, and she was only in the camp for—"

"Sue *Ellen*," Mrs. Forrest said warningly, and then could not keep from hugging this daughter she hadn't seen for such a long two weeks. "Come on, lovey," she said again to Mady, "stay with us. It's not good for you to be alone. Your momma won't be back for an hour or more yet."

Mady would not. While Mr. Forrest held the terrarium, she used her two keys to let herself into her apartment, then stood rigid until he'd put it carefully on the coffee table. He looked at her ques-

177

tioningly, patted her shoulder. "You come over whenever you want," he said.

Mady nodded.

When she was alone, she looked slowly, intently, all around her. The apartment seemed smaller than before. It seemed tight and squeezed and closed in. It looked—it looked *wizened*.

"I hate it!" she cried aloud. "I hate this place and this city, and I don't want to be here!"

Now the tears that had only trickled all day rose and overflowed with such force that she dropped to her knees. Crouching with her arms on the sofa, turning her head from side to side, she shivered and wept for everything she loved, everything she'd left and might never see again. Maria. Ellycat. The bugle blowing in the dark. She cried for herself because this—*this* around her—was what she had and would have.

I'll *never* go back there, she said to herself in despair. There'll never be a way.

After a while, still shaken with sobs and hiccuping painfully, she went over to her terrarium and knelt beside it, staring into the tiny forest. She wished she could dwindle to a mushroom-sized girl who could live in there among the pipsissewa and wintergreen, sleeping on the moss, watching the rattlesnake orchid grow high above her.

"Momma, I don't want to be here," she moaned. "I want to be back there. Always, always . . ."

But no one can cry and not stop. In time Mady couldn't force another sob, another tear. She leaned back on the sofa, too tired to move. Too tired, finally, to remember.

Moments passed. The kitchen clock ticked away, cross as ever. *Tut-tut-tut-tut-tut,* it scolded. Auto horns and sirens were loud outside, and the boys were playing stickball in the street, yelling and cursing.

Mady looked around the room again. The zebra-striped slipcovers had all been washed and ironed. They looked fresh and bright and unwrinkled. She got to her feet. Sure enough. The only crumpled place was on the sofa where she'd leaned, twisting and crying. It was sort of damp. She tried to smooth the place out with her hands.

Momma had made the apartment look so nice, so fresh and pretty. It wasn't Momma's fault that the walls seemed to close in like the sides of a box.

Aunt Lillian had agreed that maybe she should unpack, so maybe she should. She picked up the duffel bag that was by the door and carried it to the bedroom.

At the threshold she stopped.

"Oh, my own Momma," she whispered, feeling a tide of sadness again, only this time not for herself. For her mother who worked so hard and tried to keep things nice, and didn't have a doctor to marry, and had a daughter who didn't want to come home.

179

On the windowsill, with her dolls to either side of it, was a fish bowl. Not a big fish bowl but large enough for two fan-tailed black goldfish and a water plant and a little castle with a door in it. The black goldfish were swimming dreamily around, opening and closing their mouths as if they said, *oooh, ooh, oooooh* . . .

Mady blinked, and rubbed her knuckles against her eyes, and moved across the room. There was a note propped against the fish bowl.

"Welcome Home to Mady," it said. Momma had drawn two fish on it that seemed to be standing on their tails and clapping their fins.

Mady picked up the note and put it against her cheek.

"I didn't mean it, Momma," she said softly, aloud. "I didn't . . . not really."

"Didn't mean what?"

She turned. Her mother stood just inside the bedroom door in her white uniform, looking tired, pretty, and nervous.

"Maybe you'd better not tell me, at that," she said. She did not hold out her arms, as Aunt Lillian had done. She just stood there, with a funny smile, waiting.

Suddenly Mady ran and flung her arms around this mother of hers, and felt herself held close. For a while neither of them said anything.

Then Mrs. Guthrie looked at the duffel bag. "We'd better get at *that,* don't you think?"

"Okay, Momma. Only—let's have some cocoa first. And talk. And Momma, I brought you something." She felt in her pocket for the pink-and-green lanyard, left it there, took her mother by the hand, and led her into the living room, up to the terrarium.

"That's for me?" Mrs. Guthrie breathed. Mady nodded. "But I—but *Mady.* It's the—it's the loveliest thing anybody ever gave me in my life."

Mady nodded, choking up again. She was so happy at giving this gift that it made her a little dizzy.

Delicately, carefully, Mrs. Guthrie examined each plant, and Mady named and explained each one in turn. Because of course she had made this for Momma. Just because she hadn't exactly known it before didn't make any difference. She'd made this for Momma, so she could have a share of the forest too.

They sat in the kitchen then and had cocoa and talked. They decided what to name the goldfish. Ellycat I and Ellycat II. Mrs. Guthrie said it was the most original way of naming goldfish she'd ever heard of. Mady told her about Maria and about the play and the overnight hike and how Sue Ellen had learned to swim practically better than anyone else.

181

She did not tell about Sue Ellen's book, because Sue Ellen wanted to tell about that herself. Still, she could hardly wait for Momma to see it.

Then Mady asked about the hospital, about Mr. Torrance—whose daughter, it turned out, had finally come to see him and he'd been cross as two sticks all through the visit—and about Mr. Katz and Miss Rowan, who had both gone home.

It was as cozy, as wonderful, Mady thought, as any of their midnight talks had ever been. The duffel bag was forgotten as they talked the afternoon away. And at length, hesitantly but happily, Mady said, "Momma, could I tell you something very, very private? I mean, that I've never told *any*body else before?"

"I would be proud for you to."

"Well," Mady began. "Well—you see, Momma, there's this secret place—"

After she'd told about it, she found in a peculiar way that now she was glad to be home.